PEN PALS:
BOOK THREE

P.S.
FORGET IT!

by Sharon Dennis Wyeth

A YEARLING BOOK

Published by
Dell Publishing
a division of
Bantam Doubleday Dell Publishing Group, Inc.
666 Fifth Avenue
New York, New York 10103

The trademark Yearling ® is registered in the U.S. Patent and Trademark
Office.

ISBN: 0-440-40230-1
Published by arrangement with Parachute Press, Inc.
Printed in the United States of America
October 1989
10 9 8 7 6 5 4 3 2 1
OPM

For Sheri

CHAPTER ONE

As Lisa McGreevy leaned out her dormitory window, her long dark hair blew in the spring breeze. She inhaled deeply and smelled the sweet scent of the lilac tree in front of Fox Hall. The Alma Stephens School for Girls campus looked beautiful at this time of year. Lisa's mother had gone to Alma, and, for most of her life, Lisa had dreamt about becoming a student there. So far, her freshman year had been just as great as she'd always imagined it would be.

"Hey, Shanon!" Lisa suddenly shouted back over her shoulder. "Come here quick! You have to see this!"

Lisa's roommate Shanon Davis looked up from her Shakespeare book and flipped her long brown braid over her shoulder. Unlike Lisa, Shanon had never imagined she'd be attending an expensive prep school like Alma Stephens. She was a local, or "townie," which meant that

1

she came from the nearby small town of Brighton, N.H. Her public school record had been so outstanding that last year Stephens had offered her a full scholarship. She was thrilled to be going there, but sometimes she felt a little out of her element, living and studying with so many wealthy, sophisticated girls.

"What's the matter?" she asked Lisa anxiously, hurrying to her side at the window. "Is something wrong out there?"

"Look!" Lisa said, pointing out the window. "Maggie and Dan, over there by those bushes."

Dan Griffith and Maggie Grayson were two teachers at Alma Stephens. Though the girls were supposed to call them "Mr. Griffith" and "Miss Grayson," behind their backs they were always "Dan" and "Maggie." The romance between Maggie and Dan was a matter of discussion for the entire school. The girls liked to stay up late at night wondering where the two teachers were going on their next date, what they talked about, and how serious the couple had become.

Shanon followed Lisa's glance and gave a long happy sigh. Her hazel eyes sparkled. "Oh, doesn't Maggie look pretty in that yellow and white flowery dress? I wonder where she bought it."

"Maggie may be pretty," Lisa cried. "But Dan is gorgeous! Just look at his beautiful curly hair! It's all shiny and wet like he just got out of the shower. I wonder if he's wearing after-shave lotion."

Both girls giggled as Shanon leaned farther out the window. "Can you see if they're holding hands or not?" she asked.

"I can't see that far, but I'll bet they are. And I'll bet they're going somewhere really incredible, too—like out to dinner and then dancing."

"I don't know about that," Shanon answered in her quiet, sensible way. "They're probably just going to the library to look up questions for our spring midterms."

"No way!" Lisa said, still staring out the window. "Look at the way he's smiling at her. Dan Griffith is *definitely* in love with Maggie Grayson. I think this is getting *very* serious!"

"If you want to talk about *serious*," a voice said behind them, "you should see Simmie's latest letter to *me*!"

Lisa and Shanon exchanged a quick sideways glance before they turned away from the window to look at their third suitemate, Palmer Durand. She was standing in front of the mirror, combing her long blond hair. As usual, Lisa and Shanon were thinking, no matter what they'd been talking about, Palmer always managed to turn the conversation around to herself.

Palmer was the exact image of the wealthy, sophisticated kind of girl Shanon had worried about before coming to Alma Stephens. She was tall, slender, and beautiful, and she had a closetful of expensive clothes with French labels. Yet, despite Palmer's sometimes haughty ways, Lisa and Shanon both considered her a friend. They'd learned that

3

there was a real person under those designer clothes—even though that person was often hard to find.

Just then, Amy Ho, the fourth member of the suite, bounced into the room. As usual, she was dramatically dressed in black. Today it was black leather pants and an outsized black and silver T-shirt with Joan Jett's picture on the back. Her short, punky hair was moussed up into tiny spikes that stood out around her perky face and emphasized her dark almond-shaped eyes. A startling flash of color came from her long, dangling earrings that looked like lightning bolts made out of jade.

During school hours, Miss Pryn, the Alma Stephens headmistress, enforced a strict code for dress and makeup, but in the girls' dorms, anything and everything was all right. Amy always took full advantage of this, and often topped off her outfits with exotic accessories her family brought back from their trips around the world. Amy's father was a Chinese businessman, and the Ho family had lived in a number of foreign countries, including Thailand and Australia. Now Amy's father was based in New York City, which Amy liked to claim was the most exotic place she'd ever lived!

"You haven't let us see any of Simmie's letters lately, Palmer," Amy said. "So we don't have any way of knowing exactly how 'serious' he is. What in the world has he been saying?"

"Simmie" was Simmie Randolph III, Palmer's pen pal. Last fall, the four suitemates at the all-girls boarding school had come up with the idea of advertising for pen pals from the nearby Ardsley Academy for Boys. Because their suite number was 3-D, and their dormitory was Fox Hall, they'd started out by calling themselves the Foxes of the Third Dimension. They'd received many letters in response, but had wound up choosing four Ardsley suitemates—Simmie, John Adams, Arthur Martinez, and Rob Williams—who'd mysteriously called themselves The Unknown.

Palmer gave a secretive smile. "I know I haven't shown you Simmie's letters lately," she said. "That's because they've gotten so *personal*."

"Personal like how?" Lisa asked skeptically.

"Well, like I think he might want to give me his class pin or go steady!" Palmer replied. "Like he might even be in love with me!"

Shanon and Amy looked at each other with wide eyes. "Gosh," Amy said. "Are you sure, Palmer? If it's true, it's really amazing. I mean, John's letters are friendly, but he sure never says anything about going steady!" Since Amy always shared her letters, the other Foxes knew that her pen pal always wrote serious letters filled with poetry, song lyrics, and descriptions of sporting events.

"Mars doesn't say anything about going steady either," Shanon said. Her pen pal was named Arthur Martinez, but he liked to be called "Mars." "His letters are sweet and friendly, but they don't say anything about being in love with me!"

"Well, you know Mars is a lot like you, Shanon," Palmer said in a superior tone. "He's probably just too shy to speak up. And besides, you three have to remember that none of your pen pals is as sophisticated as Simmie. Remember, he's from Florida, like I am, and we know a little bit more about the finer things in life down there. And don't forget, Simmie looks like a movie star. *And* he's getting a car as soon as he turns sixteen!"

Shanon's eyes grew dreamy. Amy gave a long, drawn-out sigh. As she listened to Palmer talk about Simmie, she felt a small pang. When the Foxes had first started writing to the Unknowns, Simmie had been *her* pen pal—until Palmer maneuvered a "trade" behind Amy's back. Though Amy knew she actually had a lot more in common with her current pen pal, John, she couldn't help feeling a little jealous when she heard Palmer talking about how good-looking and sophisticated Simmie was.

Lisa, on the other hand, didn't feel at all jealous. She gave a loud snort. "Are you positive you can really believe Simmie's letters, Palmer?" she asked. "You know, a lot of boys *say* romantic things, but it doesn't always mean they're really truly in love."

Palmer tossed her long hair, and two red spots of anger appeared on her cheeks. "Well, of course you'd say that!" she snapped. "You're just jealous because your pen pal only writes letters full of silly jokes or highbrow, brainy stuff."

Lisa's big brown eyes narrowed. "I'll admit Rob has a

good sense of humor," she said through clenched teeth, "and that his letters are intelligent. He's never mushy, but at least I know his letters are for real. I'm sure you can't say the same thing about Simmie's!"

Both Amy and Shanon sensed a real fight coming on and tried to change the subject. "Has anyone seen my softball glove?" Amy asked, rummaging through a pile of objects on the desk. "I have my first practice tomorrow afternoon."

"Does anyone want me to make some of that new instant lemon drink my mom got me?" Shanon asked at the same time. "It only has thirty calories."

But Palmer and Lisa didn't pay any attention to the other girls. "That's what *you* think, Lisa!" Palmer said. "Well, I'll show you the letters. I'll *prove* Simmie's really in love with me!" She whirled around and marched out of the sitting room into her own room. A minute later, she came back with two letters in her hand. "Just listen to this!"

Dear Palmer,
You are trully an incredible girl. I have never met anyone like you before in my life. I think about you all the time and hope you are thinking about me.

Yours forever,
Simmie

"What do you think about that?" Palmer demanded, her eyes flashing. "He said 'Yours *forever*'!"

7

Lisa, Shanon, and Amy all looked at each other and then down at the floor. "Palmer," Lisa said, "how can Simmie possibly be yours forever? You're only thirteen years old, and you've only had a few chances to meet each other. I mean, I'm sure Simmie really likes you and everything, but don't you think he might just be playing games with you or—"

"I knew you'd say that!" Palmer interrupted. "But just listen to his next letter."

Dear Palmer,

I love getting letters from you. I keep them under my pilow so they can be near me at night. I wish we could see each other more somhow.

Love,
Simmie

"I see Simmie still hasn't learned to spell very well," Shanon said, glancing over Palmer's shoulder.

"Who cares about his stupid spelling!" Palmer exploded. "It's what he's saying that matters! And he's saying that he keeps my letters under his pillow. And he signed this one 'Love.'"

"I just don't know," Lisa said doubtfully. "Rob's letters are never like that. He only writes when he has something important to say, and then his letters are really intelligent. He doesn't just keep sending me a bunch of . . . well, *slop* like that."

"Slop!" Palmer yelled. "How can you call those beautiful letters slop?"

Shanon cleared her throat. "You have to admit the letters are a little on the sentimental side, Palmer," she said quietly.

"A little?" Amy put in.

"I think he might be trying to hand you a line," Lisa said.

"Oh, you're all just jealous because my pen pal's letters are better than yours!" Palmer shouted. "Particularly you!" she said, turning on Lisa. "You're *really* jealous because my pen pal is so cool and good-looking and your pen pal is such a nerd—and so homely!"

Lisa's mouth dropped open. "Homely!" she shouted back. "Rob Williams is *not* homely! And besides, why are you always talking about how people look all the time? You know there are other things in the world besides appearance!"

"Oh yeah? Well then how come you like clothes so much? I notice you spending a lot of time picking out what outfits you want to wear."

"I didn't say there was anything wrong with liking clothes," Lisa shot back. "I just said that good looks aren't the only things to think about when you're picking a boyfriend! There are other things that are more important."

"Oh yeah?" Palmer said again. "Like what?"

"Well, like personality," Lisa said. "And common interests. And *honesty*. Rob and I are friends, and I can always *believe* what he's telling me!"

"Are you calling Simmie a liar?" Palmer said shrilly.

Lisa was about to answer, but before the fight could go on, the door to the room was flung open. Kate Majors, the upperclassman in charge of the floor, came into the room and glared at the girls.

"*What* is going on in here?" she asked. "I was trying to make a phone call way down at the other end of the hall, and I could hardly hear the operator. *That's* how much noise you four were making in here!" She turned to look at Shanon. "I'm particularly surprised at you, Shanon," she said sternly. "I've never known you to do a lot of yelling and screaming."

Kate and Shanon both worked on the school newspaper and had gotten to know each other fairly well during the year. Although many of the girls thought Kate was prim, bossy, and too strict, Shanon had come to respect her.

Now Shanon felt her face growing red with embarrassment. "I'm sorry, Kate," she said in a small voice. "We didn't mean to bother anyone."

"Right, Kate," said Amy. "We're sorry. It won't happen again."

"Well, see that it doesn't!" Kate snapped. "Why am I always having problems with this suite? You know if a particular suite gets too rowdy, it's just possible that that suite might be split up before the end of the year!"

As Kate abruptly turned and left the room, Amy and

Shanon both gasped with dismay. Split up the Foxes? What a horrible idea!

Lisa looked sorry and embarrassed, too. "Sorry, Palmer," she muttered. "I didn't mean to start a fight." She waited for Palmer to apologize, but Palmer didn't say a word. Finally, Lisa turned around and went into the bedroom she shared with Shanon.

Palmer stood in the middle of the sitting room, her blue eyes still blazing with anger. "Simmie *does* love me," she muttered to Amy and Shanon. "Lisa is just a jealous little witch!"

CHAPTER TWO

When Lisa came in from crew practice a few days later, her face was flushed from both exercise and excitement. She loved rowing on the river with the other girls on the team. As she pulled off her sweater, she realized she was in a great mood. It seemed as if her fight with Palmer had happened a long time ago, and Lisa was doing her best to forget all about it. Today was not a day to dwell on a stupid old argument. Today there was good news for the Foxes.

"Hey, Shanon!" she yelled cheerfully. "We've got letters from Rob and Mars. I picked them up from our boxes after crew!"

Shanon looked up from the volume of Shakespearean sonnets she was studying for Mr. Griffith's English class. She stretched and reached out for her letter. Just then, Amy came into the sitting room. She was still wearing the sweatpants and T-shirt she'd worn to softball practice. Her cheeks were glowing from running around outside in the warm sun.

"You two got letters from your pen pals?" she said jealously when she saw the envelopes in Lisa's hands. She held up a pale blue overseas airmail envelope. "I got one from my friend Evon in Australia today, but nothing from John. Evon wants me to get her an Elvis Presley poster. You know, they're sort of collectors' items down there."

"I think I saw some at the shop called Memorabilia on Main Street last week," Lisa said.

"Terrific," said Amy. "I'll pick one up when I take my next town trip." Amy perched on the arm of the couch. "Let's hear your letters!"

"Shouldn't we wait for Palmer?" Lisa asked.

When the Foxes had first started writing to The Unknown last fall, they'd made it a policy to read their letters out loud to each other. They still liked to share their letters most of the time, though lately Palmer had been keeping Simmie's letters to herself. "If Palmer wants to hear them later, you can read them to her again," Amy said, pulling her sweaty T-shirt over her head and slipping a fresh one on. "I can't wait that long!"

"I'll go first," Shanon said breathlessly as she ripped open her envelope.

Dear Shanon,
Thank you for your last letter. Knowing I might hear

13

from you makes checking my mailbox the high point of my day! There's not much news from Ardsley lately, unless you're interested in "secret societies." What are those, pray tell? you say. Well, the name sounds a little cloak-and-dagger, but as far as I can tell, they're really just a bunch of old sports clubs that have now turned into exclusive social clubs as well. The clubs died out for a while, but for some reason (which I personally can't understand!) they've come back to life this spring. Not surprisingly, none of the societies has shown any interest in your humble servant, me (I guess I'm just not the secret society type!), though I'm pretty sure Rob and Simmie have both been "tapped," as they say, but by different clubs. All this makes for a lot of whispering and secret phone calls, etc., etc., and sometimes I feel like I'm living with a bunch of secret agents around here!

Anyway, that's all the news I have for now. Write back soon and let me know what's up with you and the other Foxes.

Your pen pal,
Mars

P.S. When you get a chance, do you think you could send me another picture of you? The old one is getting wrinkled from being handled so much!

Shanon smiled and felt her face grow warm as she read Mars' P.S. "Wow!" she said, looking up from the letter. "Secret societies! I wonder what they're like?"

14

"Me, too," said Amy. "I suppose they're sort of like fraternities in colleges. It might be kind of fun to be in one. But I know Miss Pryn would never allow anything like that at Alma Stephens!"

"Never *ever*," Shanon agreed. "Do you suppose they have rush week and hazing and initiations? I don't think I could stand the pressure."

"I think my brother Reggie told me about being tapped by a society last year," Lisa said. "I can't remember if he joined or not, but I thought it sounded pretty silly. I mean, if you know who your friends are, why can't you just go hang out with them? Why do you have to organize everybody into different clubs that keep other people out?" She looked down at Rob's letter and frowned. "I wonder why Rob hasn't ever written anything to me about these clubs—especially if he's been tapped like Mars said."

"Well, maybe he'll tell you about it in this letter," Amy said eagerly. "Open it up!"

"Okay," Lisa agreed with a smile. She was excited as she opened Rob's letter, but disappointed when she saw it was only a few lines long.

Dear Lisa,
Yo, number one Fox. Sorry this has to be so short, but my hand is so tired from writing history notes, I'm afraid my fingers are going to fall off if I write much more! (Do you also have the thrill of midterm exams to look forward to?) Anyway, I wanted to let you know I probably won't

be writing for the next couple of weeks because I'll be tied up with something. In the meantime, have fun and take care of yourself.

> *Don't forget me,*
> *Rob*

P.S. I will be thinking about you!

"Gosh, Lisa," Shanon said. "That's really a sweet letter. But I wonder why he didn't even mention the secret societies!"

"*I* wonder why he didn't tell you what he's going to be 'tied up' with!" Palmer said. She'd come through the door a moment before, just in time to hear the tail end of Rob's letter.

Lisa glanced at the letter again. "Well, he says he's been busy studying for midterms," she said thoughtfully. "He probably means he'll be working too hard to write."

Palmer grabbed the letter out of Lisa's hand and read it to herself. "I don't think that's what he means at all," she said confidently. "He starts out talking about studying, but then he changes the subject and says he'll be tied up with 'something' entirely different. It sounds very mysterious to me . . . almost as if he's deliberately keeping something from you!"

"Well, he doesn't have to tell me absolutely everything he does!" Lisa replied hotly. "Just because we're pen pals, that doesn't mean we can't have some privacy!"

16

"Oh, of course not," Palmer answered, flipping Rob's letter onto the desk. "It's just that you're always going on about what good *friends* you and Rob are, and how *honest* you are with each other, that's all. If he's so honest, why can't he tell you what's going to be keeping him 'tied up' for so long?"

"Maybe it isn't important," Lisa shot back. "Or maybe he thought I wouldn't be interested. Or maybe he just doesn't want to talk about whatever it is. Or maybe . . ."

Lisa stopped defending Rob when she realized Palmer had already left the sitting room and gone into the bedroom she shared with Amy. She sat down in the nearest chair and read Rob's letter for a third time. It *was* a sweet letter, she thought with a smile. But then she frowned. She had to admit Palmer did have a point. What could Rob possibly be doing that would keep him tied up for two or three whole weeks? And why in the world couldn't he tell her what it was?

CHAPTER THREE

Dear Lisa,

My own sweet Fox! Though I know I told you I wouldn't have a chance to write for a while, my thoughts kept drifting towardxx you so often that I couldn't help myself. I had to write you or lose my mind dreamingx about you all the time, day and night. And believe me, you adorable girl, my dreams are truly acsquisit. If I told you about them, you might actually be embarassed. They would bring a blush to your soft, gorgous face.

In fact, sweet Fox, I'm writing to ask you to meet me in town in person if you possibly can. Come to the ice creamxx parlor on Saturday at 2:00. I have something to give you that I'm positive you'll reallyy treasure. And besides, I just can't wait for a chance to lookx deeply into your beutiful eyes once more.

> *Please don't disappoint me,*
> *Rob*

P.S. Please excuse all the typing mistakes. I am not much of a typst.

When Lisa finished reading Rob's letter, there was a minute of hushed silence in the suite. Then Shanon expressed all the girls' thoughts with one word. "Wow!" she gushed.

"You can say that again," Amy said. "That letter is so hot, I'm surprised your hand isn't on fire, Lisa!"

"It's incredible, isn't it?" Lisa agreed breathlessly. "Something must have come over Rob all of a sudden. I mean this letter is so intense, I almost can't believe it's from the same person who's been writing me all year! Look—he even typed it. I wonder what that means. He's right. He's a crummy typist."

Shanon went to Lisa's side and looked over her shoulder at the letter. "He sure is," she said, giggling. "And he doesn't usually misspell all those words, does he? Look at 'beautiful' and 'gorgeous.' And what do you suppose 'acsquisit' means?" She reached for her dictionary and tried to look it up. "It's not even in here!"

"Those aren't spelling mistakes," Lisa said defensively. "They're typing errors. He just hit the wrong keys, that's all."

"I don't know what 'acsquisit' means, but I'll bet it's something nice," Amy said. "It's probably a word from some Old English poem. I mean, the whole letter is like a

19

poem. 'Bring a blush to your soft, gorgeous face.' If John wrote me something like that, I'd pass out!"

"I'd feel the same way if Mars told me he'd been dreaming about me day and night," Shanon put in, still reading over Lisa's shoulder. "What do you suppose he wants to give you in town on Saturday, Lisa?"

"I have no idea, but I sure plan to find out!" Lisa declared excitedly. "I mean, after getting a letter like this, how could I *not* go meet him in town?"

"Oh, I don't know." Palmer spoke for the first time. She'd been quietly filing her nails in the corner during the entire discussion. "I'm not sure it's such a great letter. I wouldn't get that excited about it if I were you."

Shanon, Amy, and Lisa all gaped at Palmer in amazement. "What are you talking about, Palmer?" Lisa demanded. "It's a fantastic, incredible letter!"

Palmer covered a huge, exaggerated yawn. "Oh, you know, Lisa. Sometimes people say things they don't really mean. Don't you think this letter is a bit on the sentimental side? Almost like Rob might be 'handing you a line'?"

Lisa's face turned red with anger. "How can you say something like that, Palmer!" she said heatedly. "Rob's the most truthful person in the world! He'd never stoop to something that dishonest."

Palmer tossed her hair. "Oh, so it's okay for Rob to write 'slop,' but when Simmie does it, he's a liar? Rob is so wonderful, you just automatically believe everything he tells you?"

20

Lisa thought about Palmer's words for a moment. "Okay, Palmer," she conceded. "I can see what you're getting at. Maybe I was sort of unfair about Simmie."

Palmer gave Lisa a huge smile. "That's all I wanted to hear. Now forget everything I said, Lisa. I think Rob's letter is awesome. And I think you absolutely have to go meet him in town on Saturday! There's no way you can stand him up after getting a letter like that."

Lisa was glad to have the argument come to an end. With a feeling of relief, she smiled back at Palmer.

"If you really want to go, you'll have to get permission from Kate Majors, I guess," Shanon reminded Lisa. "Remember, you're allowed to go to town to run errands if another girl goes with you—and you know I'd *love* to come and be your chaperone!"

All at once, Lisa's good mood came rushing back. "Come on then!" she said excitedly. "What are we waiting for? Let's go ask Kate right now!"

She grabbed Shanon's hand and hauled her out the door and down the hall to Kate's room. The two girls knocked on Kate's door and, without waiting for an answer, hurried into her room.

Kate was sitting at her desk, hunched over a thick math book. When Lisa and Shanon burst in, she looked up at them over the tops of her glasses. Tucking a wisp of hair behind her ear, she put down her pencil and said, "Where I come from, it's the custom to wait for a response after you knock on someone's door!"

21

Shanon turned red. "Sorry, Kate."

"Right, sorry, Kate," Lisa said, all in a rush. "It's just that we're really in a hurry because you see I absolutely have to go into town on Saturday to do some really important errands, and Shanon says she'll go with me, so I was wondering if it would be okay with you."

Kate pushed her glasses up on her nose. Slowly and deliberately, she closed her book. "Wasn't your last town trip only a few weeks ago? You know you're only allowed three trips per semester. If you use them all up, you'll be stuck on campus till June!"

"I know," Lisa answered without hesitating. "But I want to go anyway. Come on, Kate. Please say yes!"

"Well, I guess it's all right with me," Kate said. "But you'll have to check with Miss Grayson. That's Miss Pryn's new policy. All town trips have to be cleared with the dorm's resident faculty member."

Shanon caught the flash of anger in Lisa's dark eyes and pushed her toward the doorway before she could say anything. "Thanks, Kate," she said quickly. "We'll go see Miss Grayson right away."

Out in the hallway, Lisa's face was stormy. "That's just like that power-hungry Kate Majors!" she complained. "She practically makes me get down on my knees and beg her for permission to go to town. And *then* she tells me it isn't even up to her anymore!"

"Oh, don't be so hard on Kate," Shanon said soothingly. "She's just always worried about doing the right thing, that's all. I guess somebody has to remember all the rules around here!"

The two girls reached Maggie Grayson's apartment just as she was going out the door. The sweet fragrance of delicate French perfume drifted through the air. Shanon and Lisa were both sure Miss Grayson was headed out for a date with Mr. Griffith.

"Miss Grayson!" Lisa said. "We have to ask you something."

Miss Grayson glanced down at her watch. "Well, I was just on my way to meet someone . . ." she explained.

Shanon and Lisa shot each other a quick glance. They knew they were right—Miss Grayson was on her way to meet Mr. Griffith!

"Please," Lisa said urgently. "This will only take a minute. And it's really important!"

Miss Grayson looked at Lisa's flushed face and shining eyes. Then she smiled and opened her door again. "All right, you two," she said. "Come inside and tell me what's so important it can't wait."

Shanon and Lisa hurried into Miss Grayson's room and closed the door behind them. Shanon took a minute to admire the teacher's pretty pictures, colorful curtains, and soft, comfortable furniture. But Lisa wasn't wasting any time.

"I need permission to go on a town trip to run errands Saturday," she announced. "Shanon says she'll go with me. So is it okay?"

Miss Grayson gave Lisa a long, hard look. "That's what all this excitement is about?" she asked quietly. "Just a simple trip into town?"

Shanon looked down at the floor, but Lisa looked Miss Grayson right in the eye. "That's it," she said firmly. "I have a lot of really important errands. So is it all right if I go?"

Miss Grayson went to her desk and checked a record book. "Well, you do have one town trip left," she said. "So it's all right with me. But be sure you're only gone for two hours. And remember, you have to sign in and out with Kate Majors."

Lisa ran forward and hugged Miss Grayson so hard the two of them almost fell over. "Thank you, Miss Grayson!" she exclaimed.

"You're welcome," Miss Grayson said in surprise. She looked at her watch again. "And now, if you'll excuse me, I really do have to meet my friend."

Lisa and Shanon both smiled as they backed out the door. "Of course, Mag . . . er . . . Miss Grayson," Lisa said, trying not to giggle. "You wouldn't want to keep your *friend* waiting."

When their teacher was gone, Lisa and Shanon both laughed. "Did you smell that perfume she had on?" Shanon said. "I'll bet it cost a million dollars an ounce. I'm positive she's going to meet Mr. Griffith!"

"And I'm going to meet Rob!" Lisa said. "I can hardly wait till Saturday!"

Lisa's happy mood was contagious, but Shanon frowned as they walked back to their suite. "I wish we could have told her the truth about that," she said slowly. "I feel really bad that we lied about why we were going into town."

"I could never tell her I was going to meet a boy!" Lisa exclaimed. *Going to meet a boy*. Lisa liked the way it sounded. It was so wonderful—so romantic!

CHAPTER FOUR

The rest of the week went very slowly for Lisa. All she could think or talk about was her latest letter. Sometimes when she thought about it, she became puzzled. Why had Rob suddenly decided to pour out all those feelings for her? she wondered. Why had he said he'd be too busy to write, and then sent her a letter the very next day?

Most of the time, though, she didn't ask herself those questions. She told herself that getting such a romantic letter was just about the most exciting thing that had ever happened in her life. She could hardly wait to see what was going to happen on Saturday afternoon.

Even during classes, she stared out the window and daydreamed about Saturday. Once, when Mr. Griffith asked her where Shakespeare was born, she answered, "Stratford-on-Ardsley!"

Even though her roommates were also curious about what would happen Saturday, by Friday morning they were getting a little tired of the subject. That afternoon after classes, Amy looked up from *her* volume of Shakespearean sonnets. "I just can't seem to memorize one of these," she said in exasperation. "You'd think my having lived in England might have helped me handle Shakespeare a bit better, but it certainly hasn't! Why don't we go outside for a while and clear our brains? Lisa? Did you hear me?"

"What did you say?" Lisa asked dreamily.

"I *said* let's go outside for a while. Come on! It's a beautiful day." She put on her softball glove. "And I need practice with my fielding. You can hit me some fly balls."

"I'm not really in the mood for softball, Amy. And even when I *am* in the mood, I'm not very good at it! I was the strike-out queen of my old school!"

"Come on," Amy pleaded. "I'm not asking you to hit a home run. Just toss up the ball and hit it out to me. It'll be fun. And besides, it will take your mind off . . . things."

"That's just the point!" Lisa replied, laughing, as she grabbed her jacket and followed Amy out the door. "I don't *want* to take my mind off 'things.' I like thinking about Rob's letter all the time."

"I don't blame you," Amy said. "That letter really was awesome. I don't know what I'd do if I ever got something like that!"

27

"It was incredible, wasn't it?" Lisa went on. "And what if Rob wants to give me his freshman class pin or something like that?"

"What would you do? Would you accept it?" asked Amy, bounding down the front steps of Fox Hall ahead of Lisa.

"I don't know," Lisa said as she caught up with Amy at the bottom of the steps. "I know Rob is the nicest, best-looking boy I've ever met. But I'm sure my parents wouldn't like me to be wearing his ring. Or my big brother, Reggie, either, for that matter. They'd all say I was too young to go steady, blah, blah, blah. But then, they wouldn't have to know about it, would they?"

"I guess not," Amy said doubtfully. "Though I think it would be pretty hard to keep something like that a secret around here."

They continued to talk about Rob as they crossed the campus. When they reached the softball diamond, Amy handed Lisa a bat and ball and ran out to center field. "Come on, Lisa!" she called. "Hit me a few out here!"

Lisa dutifully picked up the bat and tossed the ball into the air. After ten strikes, she shook her head. "It's no use, Amy," she called. "I just can't concentrate on this!"

Amy sighed and trotted back in from the field. "That's okay," she said. "I guess I'll have to ask one of my teammates to help me practice."

The girls went back into Fox Hall and started getting ready for dinner. But, though they all dutifully went to the dining room and sat down at their table, three hours later they were hungry again.

"Let's order pizza from Figaro's," Shanon suggested. "I'm dying of hunger!"

"Me too," said Amy. "I can't stand it when Mrs. Butter makes one of her traditional English dinners like that," she added, using the girls' affectionate nickname for the school's rolypoly English cook, Mrs. Worth.

"I know what you mean," Lisa agreed. "I don't really mind her steak and kidney pie, but her treacle and suet pudding is enough to make you barf!"

The girls all laughed. Mrs. Worth adored the girls at the school, whom she fondly referred to as her "lovies." The girls loved her too, and none of them had the heart to tell her how much they disliked some of her favorite recipes.

"Pizza is the only thing that will save us from starvation," said Shanon firmly. "Let's get a deep-dish Monstro Sicilian with everything on it."

"Everything but anchovies," Lisa protested. "Those greasy little things remind me of worms!"

Half an hour later, the girls were gathered around an open pizza box in the middle of the sitting-room floor. They'd been talking about music, clothes, and food, but finally, Amy brought up the subject they were all most interested in.

"What are you going to wear when you meet Rob tomorrow, Lisa?" she asked, biting into a thick slice loaded with mushrooms, pepperoni, and sausage.

"I can't decide," Lisa said, reaching for her third piece of pizza. "My mom sent me a bunch of new T-shirts in really hot colors. I think I'll put a couple of them together and wear them with my new striped bike pants. That is, if I can still fit into them after pigging out like this!"

"That sounds cool," Shanon said. "I think Rob will really love that outfit, don't you Palmer?"

Palmer licked tomato sauce off her fingers and smiled. "Sounds good to me," she murmured.

The girls finished the pizza, cleaned up the greasy box, and got ready for bed. Lisa had a hard time falling asleep, but after several restless hours, she finally drifted off. During the night she dreamed she was going through her closet, endlessly searching for shoes to wear for her meeting with Rob. When she finally found a pair that matched, she was already two hours late.

By the time the sun came streaming through the window on Saturday morning, she'd been lying on her pillow with her eyes wide open for a whole hour. She bounced out of bed and hurried over to wake up Shanon. Shanon opened her eyes, looked at the clock, and saw that it was only 6:00 a.m.! "I'm going back to sleep," she groaned. "And I'm planning to read *A Midsummer Night's Dream* all morning long. I'll meet you in the bike room at one-thirty and not a minute sooner!"

Lisa spent the rest of the morning staring at her books, daydreaming and pretending to study. Every time she looked at her watch, only another minute had gone by. Finally, though, it really was one-thirty—time to leave for town. Lisa and Shanon went down to the bike room in the basement to take out their bikes. Shanon opened the lock on the streamlined silver bike Palmer had lent her, while Lisa got out her own ten-speed.

"Gosh," Shanon said as they pedaled out toward the road to town. "This bike is *super*! It's so smooth and powerful, I feel like I'm riding a Rolls-Royce! It was really nice of Palmer to let me borrow it since mine needs a new tire."

"I know," Lisa said over her shoulder. "Palmer can be really nice sometimes. I'm glad the two of us aren't fighting anymore."

The girls rode quickly, and they reached town in record time. They locked up their bikes in a stand near the village green and hurried to the ice cream parlor.

"We're early," Lisa said, glancing at her watch. "It's only ten minutes to two."

"We can go over those sonnets we were supposed to memorize," Shanon suggested. She pulled a paperback copy of Shakespeare's sonnets out of her back pocket. "Check me on number one-sixteen, okay? 'Let me not to the marriage of true minds admit impediments. Love is not love which alters when it alteration finds . . .'"

Lisa made a face, but she patiently read along in the book as Shanon recited three sonnets. The next time she

31

looked down at her watch, it was ten minutes after two.

"Rob's late," she said anxiously.

"Only by ten minutes," Shanon reassured her. "Did his letter say to meet him inside or outside the ice cream parlor?"

"It didn't say," Lisa said. "Maybe he's been inside waiting this whole time! I'd better go inside and check." She hurried into the ice cream parlor, but came right back out again. "He's not in there," she said.

"Well, let's wait out here a few more minutes," Shanon suggested.

"Should I go inside and get us ice cream cones?" Lisa asked. "They have those great waffle cones dipped in chocolate—plus a lot of different kinds of toppings."

"I don't know," Shanon said doubtfully. "If I eat chocolate, my face will break out." Then she smiled. "Of course, I *could* eat a tutti-fruiti peppermint cone," she added.

"I'll get myself a frozen yogurt," Lisa said. "That way I won't gain five pounds!"

She went back into the ice cream parlor and came out a few minutes later with two cones. The girls stood on the sidewalk, eating their snacks. Then Lisa looked at her watch again.

"Shanon," she said anxiously, "it's already a quarter to three!"

"Well, maybe Rob got tied up somewhere," Shanon

said. "Maybe he couldn't get permission to come into town. Maybe Ardsley has a rule about town trips, too, and he'd already used up all of his."

"Maybe," Lisa said doubtfully. "Or maybe he chickened out. Maybe he just didn't feel like showing up."

"Oh I don't believe that," Shanon said. "But we can't wait too much longer, or we'll be late going back to school. After that big deal we made about this trip, I'm afraid Kate will be watching the clock."

"Like a hawk!" Lisa agreed. "I'd better run to the store and buy something so she and Maggie will believe my story about running errands."

She hurried down the street to the drugstore, where she bought a new lip gloss for herself, a fashion magazine for Palmer, and a paperback book of crossword puzzles for Shanon. On her way out, she noticed that the little shop called Memorabilia was right next door. She went inside and bought an Elvis Presley poster and an Elvis Presley button for Amy to send to her pen pal in Australia.

Suddenly she was positive Rob must have shown up at the ice cream parlor by now. But when she rushed back there, Shanon just looked at her and shook her head "no." Lisa felt so disappointed, she couldn't say a word. In total gloomy silence, the two girls trudged to the village green, unlocked their bikes, and headed back to school.

When they walked into their suite, Amy was waiting for them, bubbling over with excitement. She was dying to hear about the meeting with Rob. She started to ask a question, but the instant she saw Lisa's sad face, she abruptly closed her mouth.

Just then, Palmer hurried into the room. "You're back!" she exclaimed eagerly. "How did it go with Rob?"

Lisa just shook her head. All at once, she felt like being alone and having a good cry. But Palmer didn't take the hint that something was wrong.

"Well, what did Rob want?" she asked.

"Nothing," Lisa said glumly. "He didn't even come."

"No kidding!" Palmer said, sounding surprised. "Who would have expected that?"

"Oh Lisa!" Amy said sympathetically. "That's really rough. You must feel awful."

"You guessed it," Lisa said, with a feeble attempt at a smile.

"Maybe he got a flat tire on his bike or something," Amy said. "Or maybe he got tied up at school."

"Or *maybe* he wasn't being entirely truthful with you," Palmer said pointedly. "Maybe Rob never intended to show up!"

"Stop it, Palmer!" Shanon snapped. "Lisa's feeling bad enough as it is. You don't have to make her feel worse!"

"Shanon's right, Palmer," Amy said. "I'm sure Rob had a really good reason for not showing up in town. After all, why would he do a mean thing like purposely *not* showing up?"

"How should I know?" Palmer asked. "All I know is

34

that that *is* exactly what happened. Rob said he'd do one thing, and then he did just the opposite. Why is Lisa 'just being helpful' when she says she thinks Simmie is a phony, but I'm being mean when I say the same thing about a boy who just stood her up?"

Lisa glared at Palmer. "Stop it!" she said. "You're only saying this stuff because you're still mad about what I said about Simmie's letters before! I thought we'd settled all that!"

"Maybe I *am* still mad. But that doesn't change anything. What I'm saying is still the truth!" Palmer said, her voice getting louder with each word.

Lisa stared at Palmer and blinked back hot, stinging tears. She knew Palmer was just trying to get back at her for criticizing Simmie, but the other girl's words still hurt her feelings, and they still just *might* be the truth. Angry and upset as she was, Lisa couldn't stop asking herself the same questions Palmer was asking: Why *had* Rob told her to meet him in town and then not shown up? Had he really been delayed by something he couldn't help? Or was he being dishonest, playing with her feelings—"handing her a line"?

CHAPTER FIVE

———————◆———————

Tuesday morning Amy found four letters from The Unknown in the Foxes' mailboxes. As soon as classes were over, she ran back to the room with them. "Mail call!" she cried happily. "Today all four of us got letters!"

Palmer, Amy, and Lisa hurried into the sitting room to get their letters. In what was getting to be her habit, Palmer grabbed Simmie's letter from Shanon and then hurried to the bedroom to read it by herself. The other girls watched her go and then looked at each other.

"She's really taking the fun out of the pen pals," Lisa complained. "When we started writing letters last fall, we all agreed to share them with each other!"

"Shhhh," Shanon said. "She'll hear you!"

"I don't care if she does!" Amy said loudly. "She's been acting really obnoxious lately, and somebody ought to tell her to just knock it off."

36

"Maybe she'll change her mind later and let us see her letter," Shanon said. "But for now, Lisa, why don't you go ahead and read yours? I'm dying to know why Rob didn't show up on Saturday. I'll bet he has a really good excuse."

Lisa shook her head. "I'm too nervous to read it," she confessed. "You go first, Amy."

"Okay," Amy said. "Here goes."

Dear Amy,

I thought you might want to read my latest poem. Maybe you'll want to put it to music, and we can write another song together the way we did last winter.

> *Secrets in the air,*
> *Private thoughts hidden,*
> *Rich smells outside,*
> *I in the middle,*
> *Noises in the night,*
> *Green, blooming trees.*

To tell you the truth, I'm not exactly sure what it means myself. I'm just trying to describe what's going on around me, I guess. But anyway, I hope you like it.

Write back soon,
John
P.S. Do Foxes get restless at this time of year? I sure do!

Amy's face was puzzled when she looked up from the letter. "If you read down the first letters of each line, it spells 'spring,' " she said. "I'm not sure what else the poem means. It sounds sort of mysterious! But I like it."

"I do, too," Shanon said. "I think John's poetry is really getting better. Listen to what Mars says in his letter."

Dear Shanon,

This place is getting beyond weird lately. Remember those "secret societies" I wrote you about? Well, they're really going wild right now. They have unbelievable names, like The Ultra Cools and The Bods. And they have guys doing crazy stunts you wouldn't believe! For instance, yesterday all the guys who wanted to get into The Ultra Cools had to run around all day with their underwear on—on top of their clothes! And the would-be Bods weren't allowed to use any silverware during dinner. You should have seen those slobs in the dining room last night, trying to eat with their hands! It was a total gross-out, particularly because the main course was split-pea soup! Most of this stuff is pretty good for a laugh, but some of the stunts strike me as being kind of mean—like when they try to make some guys look dumb. Every night I thank my lucky stars I'm not trying to get into one of those societies.

To change the subject to something more pleasant, I wanted you to know I like Shakespeare's sonnets, too, particularly number 18. Think of me when you read it!

Your pen pal,
Mars

Shanon looked up from the letter and sighed.

"Come on, Shanon," Amy said. "Go look up sonnet eighteen."

"I don't have to," Shanon breathed. "I know it by heart. It's the one that starts: 'Shall I compare thee to a summer's day?' It's *my* favorite, too!"

"Wow!" Amy exclaimed. "Spring fever is making *all* the Unknowns sound romantic." She looked over at Lisa. "Come on, Lisa, it's your turn, and you haven't even opened your envelope yet!"

Lisa tried to smile. "I'm scared to," she admitted. "What if Rob says he didn't come to town Saturday because he hates me or something?"

"Don't be silly," Shanon said. "If he hated you, why would he be bothering to write you?"

"Okay," Lisa said. "I guess you're right." She took a deep breath and ripped open her envelope.

My dear angelic fox, Lisa,
Can you forgive me? If you are angry with me, I shall drown in dispair. I am too lowly to kiss the bottom of your delacate feetx.

Lisa stopped reading for a minute and gaped at Amy and Shanon. "Gosh," she said. "Rob must be taking lessons from John or something. He never used such poetic language before!"

"He must be taking spelling lessons from Simmie,"

Shanon joked, glancing over Lisa's shoulder. "He never made so many mistakes before!"

"I guess he still isn't used to the typewriter," Lisa said. "I wonder why he's started typing his letters all of a sudden like this."

"Maybe he wants to practice typing," Shanon suggested practically. "He sure needs to practice."

"Go *on*, Lisa!" Amy urged. "What else does he say about Saturday."

I was on my way to meet you Saturday when my bike got a flat tire! #Naturally, desparate as I was to meet you, I raced to the next gas station to get the tire patched. Unfortunatly, it took forever, and by the time I got there, you'dx already given up on me. Can you forgive me, oh fair one¢

Lisa looked up from the letter again. "Oh fair one?" she repeated. "Now he's starting to sound like one of Shanon's sonnets!"

"I think it's romantic," Shanon said. "Hurry up and read the rest of the letter."

I feel it isn't fair for me to keep you wonderingg about what it was I wanted to give you. As you may have guessed, it was my dearest possexsion—my freshman classs pin! I want you to wear it always. Will you meet me by the boathouse on the girls' grounds next Saturday? I know it's risky, but I can't wait any longer for you to have my pin! Please be there at 1:00. This time I won't dissapoint you!

Your pin pal,
Rob

When Lisa finished the letter, she let out a long breath. "Well, I guess he doesn't hate me," she smiled.

"I guess not!" Amy agreed. "It sounds like just the opposite!"

But Shanon was frowning. "I don't like this, Lisa," she said. "Rob's asking you to do something that's against the rules. You could really get into trouble. You know we're not allowed to have visitors without special permission—particularly not boys. If you got caught, you might even get suspended!"

"Oh, don't be silly, Shanon. She'd never get caught!"

Lisa, Amy, and Shanon looked up from their letters and saw that Palmer had come back into the sitting room and was listening to the conversation.

"Lisa would never get caught," she said again. "The boathouse is two miles away from the school! Nobody on the faculty ever goes way out there!"

"Still . . ." Shanon started to object.

"Besides," Palmer hurried on, "what if a teacher does see Lisa? Is it her fault she just 'happened' to be jogging by the boathouse when the Ardsley crew just 'happened' to be rowing by?"

"That's dishonest, Palmer!" Shanon exclaimed.

"Oh, only a little bit," Palmer said. She turned to Lisa. "Rob *is* on the crew team, isn't he, Lisa?"

"Yes he is!" Lisa said excitedly. "That's probably why he knows he can be at the boathouse at one!"

"Well, there you go," Palmer said. "You have the perfect cover story. What could possibly go wrong?"

"I can think of lots of things," Amy insisted. "What if the crew team is late, and a teacher sees Lisa standing around waiting by the boathouse?"

Palmer snorted. "Oh that would never happen. Why are you two trying to talk Lisa out of this?"

"We just don't want her to get into serious trouble," Amy said.

"I think the whole thing is too risky," Shanon added.

Palmer's blue eyes grew wide and innocent. "But don't you *want* Lisa to have Rob's freshman class pin? You're not jealous, are you?"

"Of course not!" Amy said heatedly. "Of course we want her to have Rob's pin. If she wants it, that is."

Amy, Shanon, and Palmer all looked at Lisa. "You do want Rob's pin, don't you, Lisa?" Palmer asked.

"I guess I do," Lisa said. "I mean, I'm positive I do. I'm just surprised at the way he's giving it to me, out of the blue. I can't figure out why he's acting like this all of a sudden. But I do know I really like him, and I'd like to have his pin."

"Well, in that case," Palmer argued, "what's your

42

problem? If you really like Rob, you'll be willing to take a small risk in order to get his pin. Right?"

"Right!" Lisa agreed with a big smile. "Now all I have to do is make it through the week till Saturday afternoon comes around again!"

CHAPTER SIX

After another long, draggy week for Lisa, Saturday finally came. At lunch, which was served at 11:30 on Saturdays, Lisa was barely able to choke down two mouthfuls of Mrs. Butter's strawberry trifle, which was normally her favorite dessert. By noon, she was back in Suite 3-D, throwing on her new fluorescent crimson and purple running pants and sweatshirt. She pulled her long hair back behind her ears and wound a purple elastic ponytail holder around it. A few minutes later, she was jogging along the path to the boathouse.

The night before, Lisa had begged the other three Foxes to follow her to the boathouse and act as lookouts in case a faculty member showed up when Rob was there. "I'm much too nervous to do this alone," she'd said. "I'll feel better if I know you guys are right behind me."

So, a few minutes after Lisa headed up the path, Amy,

Shanon, and Palmer set out in the same direction. They were all wearing brightly colored sweatsuits, too. They started off jogging, but after a while, they slowed to a walk.

"I *hate* jogging!" Palmer exclaimed. "I don't see why anybody does it!"

"It's good exercise," Amy said. "I love it. I get really warmed up after a mile or two, and then I feel like I can keep going forever."

"Maybe we should start running again," Shanon said anxiously. "Lisa might get in trouble if we're not there to warn her if a teacher comes! And she said she wanted us around when she met Rob."

"Oh, I wouldn't worry about Rob showing up before we do," Palmer said with a yawn. "Lisa was in such a rush, she's going to get there way too early."

Before long, the three girls rounded a bend in the path and saw the boathouse just ahead. They could also see Lisa, standing at the edge of the water. She was peering down the river in the direction of Ardsley Academy.

"I guess you were right, Palmer," Amy said. "Rob hasn't shown up yet."

"I told you she'd be way too early," Palmer repeated with a smile. She started looking around for a place to sit. "Let's go watch the show from that bench over there behind the bushes," she suggested. "I wouldn't want to miss a single second of *this* historic meeting."

Shanon looked nervously up and down the path. "I

suppose it's okay," she said. "I don't see anyone coming from either direction."

She and Amy followed Palmer over to a long bench that had been set up so spectators could watch the spring crew racing. Their seats gave them a good view of the river, but the bushes hid them from anyone coming along the pathway.

Amy looked down at her bright yellow plastic watch. "It's five minutes after one," she said. "Rob's late. Do you think he's going to stand Lisa up again? I can't believe anyone would do something so mean!"

"Wait a minute!" Shanon said excitedly. "Isn't that a boat coming up the river?"

Palmer got to her feet and peered in the direction Shanon was pointing. Then she gave another smile. "You're right," she said. "Four people in a boat. *Definitely* male!" She started creeping up toward the water. "Let's get a little closer."

Shanon tugged at Palmer's sleeve. "Wait a minute," she whispered angrily. "They'll see us. Besides, Lisa wants us to *watch* her—not stand right next to her! Rob doesn't want to give the three of *us* his class pin!"

Palmer shook off Shanon's hand. "Will you stop being such a worrier? I'm not trying to horn in on the action. I just want to see what's going on!"

Shanon and Amy looked at each other with raised eyebrows. Then they shrugged and tiptoed after Palmer, as she walked closer to the boathouse. The three of them came to a stop behind an enormous oak tree only a few yards away from Lisa.

"The boat's coming!" Amy whispered. "Rob's here!"

Shanon stuck her head out from behind the tree and looked at the boat. Then she frowned. "Hey!" she said. "Rob's not in that boat! I don't recognize three of the guys, though they look like upperclassmen to me. But I think . . . yes, I'm right! Isn't that Simmie sitting in the middle?"

Palmer stared at the boat and gave a little laugh. "Well, what do you know about that?" she said. "*My* pen pal has shown up instead of Lisa's!" She came out from behind the tree and moved even closer to the boathouse. "I guess I don't have to hide from my own pen pal! Don't you think he looks adorable with his hair all windblown like that?"

Within a few minutes, the boys had docked at the boathouse. Simmie climbed out of his seat and turned around to pick up a big box from the floor of the boat. The three strangers stayed where they were, making jokes and grinning at each other.

"Hi there, Lisa," Simmie said as he walked up to where she was standing. "Lovely afternoon, isn't it?"

"What are you doing here, Simmie?" Lisa sounded confused and upset. "Where's Rob?"

"Rob?" Simmie said. "Rob Williams? Uh . . . he couldn't make it."

"Couldn't make it? But he's the one who asked me to meet him here!"

47

"Uh . . . right," Simmie said. He turned to his friends in the boat and smiled and waved. "Just be a minute, guys!" he called. Then he turned back to Lisa. "Uh . . . what was that you were asking me, Lisa?"

Lisa glared at him and clenched her fists. "I was asking you why exactly Rob couldn't make it after he asked me to meet him here!"

"Uh . . . right, right, of course," Simmie said hurriedly. "Well, the fact is that he was . . . he was . . . too busy, that's it. He was too busy to make it."

Lisa blinked. She couldn't believe this was happening two times in a row! It was embarrassing and downright cruel. Why was Rob doing this to her? She had to swallow hard to keep from crying right in front of everyone.

Meanwhile, Simmie was holding out the big box he'd taken from the boat. "Rob sends his apologies, of course," he said. "And he also asked me to give you this present."

Lisa took the box and stared down at it in bewilderment. What was going on? she asked herself. The box was big enough to hold a blouse or skirt—*way* too big for a class pin! *Maybe it's his letter sweater*! she thought. But, no—he'd definitely said he was sending the pin.

From their position behind the tree, Amy and Shanon looked at each other in confusion. "There's something weird about this," Amy whispered. "Something just doesn't feel right around here."

Just then, Shanon noticed that Simmie was staring right up at Palmer, who was standing a few yards in front of the

48

oak tree. While Lisa was busy examining the outside of Rob's box, Simmie gave Palmer a smile, followed by a big wink! Palmer giggled and then quickly ducked her head.

Shanon's eyes narrowed and her mouth became a thin line. She was absolutely positive Amy had hit the nail on the head. *Something* just didn't feel right around here!

CHAPTER SEVEN

After Simmie and his friends had rowed away, Lisa started back down the path with Rob's box. She was walking so fast that Shanon and Amy had to run to catch up with her. Palmer lagged behind.

Just outside Fox Hall, Miss Grayson stopped Amy and asked her to run an errand for her. Shanon and Lisa hurried upstairs to their bedroom and locked the door.

"What do you think this could be, Shanon?" Lisa asked, staring down at the present. "Rob said he wanted to give me his class pin. Why would he put that in such a huge box?"

Shanon wrapped the end of her long braid around her finger. "I'm not sure," she said thoughtfully. "It doesn't make sense to me, but I guess the only way to find out what's in there is to open up the box."

Lisa took a long breath, pulled off the top of the box, and reached inside. It *was* a sweater—a huge orange one!—but certainly not Rob's varsity sweater. "Ugh!" Lisa cried. "This is the ugliest thing I've ever seen. It's all dirty. And it even has a big hole in one sleeve!"

"Oh, Lisa," Shanon said sympathetically. "What a horrible thing to do to somebody. Why would anybody want to do something like that?"

Lisa threw the sweater across the room. All at once, she sat down on the bed and burst into tears. "Why is Rob playing all these mean tricks on me?" she sobbed in rage and frustration. "I just don't understand it. I . . . I thought he *liked* me! But even if he doesn't, he doesn't have to torture me like this! What did I ever do to him?"

Shanon sat down on the bed and put her arm around her friend. "You never did anything to him," she said. "And I don't understand it, either. It doesn't make any sense . . . unless . . . unless maybe . . ."

Before Shanon could finish, Lisa jumped to her feet. She wiped her hand across her wet face. Then her expression grew stormy with rage. "Well, I don't care why he's doing it!" she cried. "It's not funny, and I don't like it, and I'm going to tell him so!"

"Maybe you should give yourself a little time to cool off," Shanon said anxiously. "Maybe you shouldn't write Rob while you're this angry."

"I'm never going to cool off about this!" Lisa said. "It's

51

just too unforgivable! I'm going to write Rob a letter and tell him I never want anything to do with him ever again!"

And with that, she ran to the desk, yanked open the drawer, and pulled out a piece of her stationery. As she reached for a pen, she knocked over her plastic pencil cup. Pens and pencils flew across the floor and scattered into the corners, but Lisa didn't even notice.

Rob,

Probably somewhere inside your mixed-up head you have an explanation for the horrible mean things you've been doing to me, but you can keep your excuses to yourself because I don't want to hear them. In fact, I never want to hear or read another word from your dishonest mouth! Don't ever write to me or try to get in touch with me again! If I ever get another one of your lying letters, I'll burn it up!

Hatefully yours,
Lisa

While Lisa was writing, Shanon sat on the bed, feeling miserable and helpless. More than anything, she wanted to cheer up her roommate, but even though she searched her brain for ideas, she couldn't think of a single useful thing to say or do. After a while, as she sat and thought, a germ of a theory began to grow in the back of her mind. She didn't like her idea, and she wasn't sure she was right, so she didn't say anything to Lisa about it. She didn't want to make a mistake about something like this. It would be terrible if she were wrong. Unfortunately, she was almost positive she *wasn't* wrong!

When Lisa finished scrawling out her angry letter, she balled it up, then smashed it down flat and stuffed it into an envelope. She wrote Rob's name and address on the outside and got to her feet. "I'm going to mail this right away," she announced. "Before anyone tries to change my mind!"

She pushed back her desk chair and stomped out of the bedroom, with Shanon following behind. As they came into the sitting room, Palmer looked up from a chair in the corner. She was pretending to read a social studies book, but Shanon noticed it was upside down!

"Well?" Palmer said eagerly, jumping to her feet and standing right in front of Lisa. "Did you open Rob's present? What was it? I'll bet it was something really elegant and expensive, like a new silk scarf or a new pair of boots."

"You couldn't be more wrong, Palmer," Lisa said through clenched teeth. "Now if you'll excuse me, I have an errand to run!" She yanked open the door and stalked out into the hallway. As she left, she slammed the door behind her. It closed with a loud BAM!

Palmer gazed after Lisa for a few seconds. Then she

turned around and faced Shanon. Her large blue eyes had never looked more innocent.

"Wow," she said. "What in the world is bugging Lisa? She looked ready to kill someone. And she sounded like she'd been crying."

Shanon stared at Palmer and folded her arms across her chest. "You'd cry, too," she said grimly, "if someone you trusted did such a cheap, dishonest thing to you."

"She should have listened to me," Palmer said with smug satisfaction. "I *told* her she couldn't trust that Rob Williams. But would she listen? No way! All she could do was babble on about how honest he was, how sincere, how *trustworthy*."

"I'm not sure I was talking about Rob," Shanon snapped angrily, "when I said that Lisa was betrayed by someone she trusted."

Palmer's mouth dropped open in an exaggerated look of surprise. "Wha . . . well who *are* you talking about then?"

"I think you already know, Palmer! I'm talking about you!"

"Me!" Palmer cried. "You can't be talking about me, Shanon! *I'm* not the one who sent Lisa a dirty old sweater!"

"Aha!" Shanon took a step forward and glared at Palmer. "How did you know there was a sweater in that box, Palmer? Lisa just opened it a few minutes ago. And I'm the only one who saw what was inside!"

Palmer stepped backwards. As she realized what a big

mistake she'd just made, her face flooded with color. Unable to meet Shanon's outraged gaze, she guiltily stared down at the floor.

Something else occurred to Shanon, and her voice got even louder as she cried, "You were behind Lisa's trip to town last week, too, weren't you?"

"I was not!" Palmer insisted. "I—"

But, before Palmer could say anything else, the door opened and Amy hurried into the sitting room. "Sorry I couldn't be here sooner," she said, "but Miss Grayson nailed me and sent me on some stupid errand to the office." She looked back over her shoulder. "I just saw Lisa heading toward Booth Hall. She looked terrible—sad and mad at the same time. What happened with that big box from Rob?"

"Maybe you should ask our dear roommate Palmer that question!" Shanon answered angrily.

Amy looked confused. "I don't understand," she said.

Shanon tapped her foot on the floor. "Tell her, Palmer. And tell me. Tell both of us the whole story."

Amy made an impatient noise. "What's going on around here," she demanded. "What could Palmer possibly know about Rob's present for Lisa?" She turned to look at Palmer. "Why do I have to hear about the box from you, Palmer?"

Palmer cleared her throat, but she was too embarrassed to say anything.

"You have to hear about the box from Palmer," Shanon

explained through clenched teeth, "because she knows more about it than anyone else. She knows because she was in on this dirty trick from the very beginning! In fact, if I'm right, the box was probably Palmer's very own idea!"

CHAPTER EIGHT

———◆———

"You're wrong!" Palmer blurted out. "At least about most of it."

"Yeah, sure," Shanon said doubtfully. "Tell that to Lisa when she comes back. She's the one you owe the explanation to."

Palmer looked down at the elegant gold watch she wore on her left wrist. "But I'm having my nails done by that girl who does manicures," she cried. "I'm already late for the appointment."

"I don't care if your nails grow into witches' claws!" Amy said. "In fact, I'm surprised they haven't already!" She moved around and blocked the doorway with her body. "I'm still pretty confused about what it is you've done, Palmer. But if you had anything to do with making Lisa so upset, I want to hear about it. I'm not letting you out of this room until you tell us all the whole story—the *true* story!"

A minute later, Amy heard footsteps in the hallway outside. She stepped away from the door so Lisa could come in.

Lisa walked into the room, rubbing her hands together with grim satisfaction. "Well, that takes care of that!" she said. "You were right about Rob from the start, Palmer. He definitely *is* a nerd. And the only thing worse than a nerd is a dishonest nerd!"

Palmer looked at Lisa, and her face grew even redder than before. "Uh . . . what exactly did you do, Lisa?" she asked in a small voice.

"I wrote that jerk a 'Dear John' letter, that's all. Only in this case it was a 'Dear Rob' letter!"

Shanon gasped in dismay. "I knew I should have stopped you before," she moaned. "But I wasn't sure what was going on then."

"I think you'd better listen to what your *friend* Palmer has to tell you now, Lisa," Amy said. She took Lisa by the arm and pulled her over to the pink loveseat. "And I think you'd better be sitting down while you hear what she has to say!"

Bewildered, Lisa allowed herself to be drawn across the room to the couch. She sat down and gave Palmer an expectant look.

Palmer was silent for a long moment. "Well, you see," she said finally, in a strangled voice, "it wasn't really my fault at all. It wasn't my idea or anything, and I hardly had anything to do with it."

Shanon and Amy snorted simultaneously, but Lisa only looked more confused than ever. "Didn't have anything to do with *what?*"

Palmer held her hand out in front of her. "Couldn't we talk about this later?" she pleaded. "The manicure girl is booked up for weeks, and if I don't show up soon, I'll lose my appointment!"

"You'll feel better if you tell her right away," Shanon said, giving Palmer a stern look.

"Right, Palmer," Amy put in. "Because if you wait much longer, Shanon and I are going to lock you in the closet and starve you till you talk!"

Lisa got to her feet and tossed her long hair back. "Will someone please tell me what we are talking about here before I go crazy?" she screamed.

"All right!" Palmer screamed back. "Just stop screaming at me!"

All four girls heard a set of footsteps come to a stop outside their door. "All we need now is that snoopy Kate Majors coming in here," Palmer said. "She's such a big busybody and—"

"Tell her now, Palmer!" Amy ordered. "Quit trying to change the subject!"

"All right," Palmer said in a quieter voice. "It's about the sweater you got from Rob, Lisa. The one that was in that big box."

"But how did *you* know what was in the box?" Lisa asked. "I only showed the sweater to Shanon, so how did you know what Rob sent me?"

"How indeed?" Amy said ominously.

"Let me finish!" Palmer said. "I knew about the sweater because Simmie told me about it. You see, the sweater isn't really from Rob at all. It's from Simmie."

Lisa fell down on the couch again. "Simmie!" she repeated. "What does Simmie have to do with me and Rob? Why would Simmie want to send me a filthy old sweater?"

"Well, you see it was all a hazing stunt. Simmie really wanted to get into one particular secret society at Ardsley. It's called The Hydraulic Dudes, and it's absolutely the most exclusive one. You can understand how it would be so important to him, can't you?"

She looked eagerly around the room, but all she saw were three angry faces. She cleared her throat and went on. "So anyway, the stunt Simmie had to perform was to embarrass one of his roommates. And since he knew that Rob was going to be away from school for a few weeks, he just—"

"Away from school!" Lisa gasped. "You mean he's not even at Ardsley right now? Then who wrote me those two letters? I could swear they had an Ardsley postmark on them!"

"Of course they did, Lisa!" Shanon explained. "But Rob's not the only boy who goes to Ardsley. Those letters weren't from Rob at all. Simmie was setting you up. He wrote those letters himself!"

"I'll bet he had some help with them," Amy said with a dark look at Palmer. "In fact, this whole stunt has your mark on it, Palmer."

"I didn't even know anything about it until the last batch of letters came. Honest!" Palmer defended herself. "When you went to town, I had no idea what was going on. But by the time Simmie's letter came telling me about the stunt, I was so angry with your superior attitude that I just let the whole boathouse thing happen without bothering to warn you."

Amy, Shanon, and Lisa gaped at each other. Amy was the first to speak. "If this isn't the meanest, most vicious, most lowdown . . ." She paused, suddenly at a loss for words.

Palmer folded her arms in front of her. "Oh, maybe it was a little mean!" she said hotly. "But it serves you right, Lisa! If you hadn't been so nasty about Simmie's letters, I never would have let you fall for this trick. Besides, what are you all making such a big deal about? We were going to tell Rob the whole thing when he got back. So nobody really got hurt, did they?"

Lisa started to make an angry reply, when all at once her face turned ghostly white. "Nobody got hurt?" she said. "What about me . . . and Rob when he gets back and sees that horrible letter I just mailed him? I told him I never wanted to see him or hear from him again! What is he

61

going to think when he reads that? Thanks a lot, Palmer! You just ruined the best relationship I've ever had in my whole life!"

For a minute, there wasn't a sound in the entire suite. Then Lisa jumped to her feet, burst into tears, and ran into her bedroom.

CHAPTER NINE

Amy glared at Palmer. "Well, are you satisfied *now*?" she asked. "Simmie was just supposed to embarrass one of his roommates. Look what you've done to one of *yours*!"

She knocked softly on Lisa's bedroom door and tiptoed inside. Lisa was lying facedown on her bed, crying into her pillow. When Amy came in, she sat up and wiped her eyes.

"Oh, Amy," she said. "What am I going to do? When Rob gets that letter I sent, he'll think I hate him. He won't want anything to do with me ever again!"

Amy perched on the edge of Lisa's bed. "All we have to do is think this thing through," she said. "There must be a way to save this situation. You say Rob's an intelligent guy, right?"

"R . . . right," Lisa sniffled. "That's one of the things I like so much about him."

"So, all you have to do is explain the whole thing to him

and he'll understand. Once he hears the whole story, he'll know it wasn't your fault!"

Lisa's tear-streaked face started to look hopeful. "You're right!" she said excitedly. "If I could just talk to him, I could tell him to tear up that letter without even reading it! I'll call him at school." She jumped to her feet, but then she frowned. "But Palmer said Rob was away from school. I *can't* call him there!"

"Maybe you could call him at home then."

"That's no good either, Amy. I don't have the slightest idea what Rob's home phone number is. All I know is that he lives in some fancy little town outside of Boston—I don't even know the name of it!"

Amy concentrated for a minute. "They have to have that information at the Ardsley office," she said thoughtfully. "Maybe if you called up over there and asked. . . ."

Lisa made a face. "It's a good idea, but I'm sure they wouldn't just hand out a boy's home phone number to any old girl who called and asked for it. I mean can you imagine Miss Pryn giving out one of our home phone numbers to a boy? If a boy phoned Stephens asking for a girl's number, she'd probably put him on hold while she got in touch with the FBI and had his call traced so she could have him arrested and thrown in jail!"

Amy smiled. "You're right," she said. "Do you suppose you could call the Ardsley office and pretend to be a parent? You know, the mother of a friend of Rob's who wants him to visit over spring break or something?"

"Hello," Lisa said in a piping falsetto. "This is Mrs. Whitmore-Remmington-Blakesmith, darling. Would you mind ever so much telling me the home phone number of one of your young lads? We're desirous of his company at our country estate over the spring holidays."

Amy laughed loudly while Lisa just smiled and shook her head. "I'm no good at stuff like that," she said. "I'd probably crack up right in the middle of the conversation."

Amy and Lisa were still giggling when Shanon came into the room. "Well, if you're laughing," she said happily, "you must be feeling a little better, Lisa."

"I'd be feeling a lot better," Lisa answered, "if I could figure out a way to get Rob's home phone number. Then I could call him up and explain about my nasty letter."

"Good idea!" Shanon exclaimed. "And I think I know where you can get his number, too. Kate Majors has an Ardsley register in her room!"

"She does?" Amy said in surprise. "What does she need an Ardsley register for?"

"I don't know what she needs it for," Shanon said. "But I know she has it. I saw it there once when I was talking to her about an article for the newspaper. It has all the boys' home numbers and addresses."

"Who cares *why* she has it!" Lisa declared. "I'm going to go ask her for Rob's phone number right now!"

"We'll come with you," Amy said.

The three girls charged out of the bedroom and headed for the hall. As they passed Palmer in the sitting room, she looked up at them expectantly, but they didn't even glance in her direction. When they were gone, she slumped back into her chair and bit her lip.

As usual, Kate Majors was at her desk, hunched over a thick book. This time, it was a history of England in the Middle Ages. When Amy, Shanon, and Lisa came into her room, Kate squinted at them over the tops of her reading glasses.

Lisa got right to the point. "Do you really have an Ardsley register in here, Kate?" she asked.

Kate stuck her pencil behind her ear. "Perhaps," she said. But her eyes slid sideways toward a blue paperback on a nearby corner bookshelf.

Without asking permission, Lisa ran to the corner and yanked the register off the shelf. Kate reached over and took it away from her. "You can't just barge in here and help yourself to my books," she said angrily. "Besides, there's confidential information in there!"

"If it's so confidential, how come you have it?" Amy asked.

Kate's thin face flushed with anger. "Because I need it, that's why. A . . . good friend of mine at Ardsley gave it to me."

Lisa, Amy, and Shanon exchanged smiles. Kate's "good friend" at Ardsley almost had to be Lisa's older brother, Reggie. Reggie and Kate had struck up a friendship last winter, and the Foxes thought the two of them might even have become pen pals.

Shanon decided to try a diplomatic approach. Even though Kate often acted like a fussbudget, Shanon knew the older girl was actually quite nice. "Kate," she said quietly, "Lisa really needs to get her pen pal's home phone number from the directory."

"Why?" Kate asked.

"That's none of your business," Lisa said hotly. "Why do you always have to—"

"Lisa and her pen pal had a misunderstanding!" Shanon broke in hastily. "If Lisa talks to him, she can explain the whole thing."

Kate shrugged and handed the directory to Lisa. "I suppose it's okay," she said. "But I hope you won't make a habit of calling your pen pal at home all the time. I'm sure his parents wouldn't appreciate it. And please don't tell *anybody* where you got his home number!"

Lisa was so busy flipping through the directory, she didn't really hear what Kate was saying. She found Rob's home address and phone number, scribbled them onto a scrap of paper, and headed for the door. "Thanks a lot, Kate," she said over her shoulder. "You saved my life!"

Back in the suite, Lisa hunted everywhere for coins to use in the pay phone. Amy and Shanon had spent their last dimes in the vending machine, but Palmer dug a pile of quarters out of her coin purse. She handed them to Lisa and waited for a "thank you," but Lisa was still too angry with Palmer to speak to her.

With the back pocket of her pants filled with change,

Lisa clinked down the hall to make her call. As she started to dial, she felt so nervous she almost dropped half the money on the floor. And when the operator came on and said, "Please deposit two dollars," she had trouble finding the correct change. Finally, she dug out the right coins. The call went through and the phone began to ring.

"Williams residence," said a formal voice.

"Uh . . . hello," Lisa squeaked. "Is this Mrs. Williams?"

"No, miss," the voice answered. "This is Mrs. Markham. The housekeeper."

"Oh," Lisa said. She was silent for a few seconds.

"Can I help you, miss?" the voice on the phone asked.

"Uh . . . yes. May I please speak to Rob Williams?"

"He's not here," said the housekeeper. "Can I take a message for him?"

Now Lisa felt completely confused. "He's not there?" she said.

"No, miss. Not right now."

"Can you tell me where he is?" Lisa asked.

"Rob's in the hospital," Mrs. Markham said. "He won't be home for a while."

"In the hospital!" Lisa cried.

"Yes, that's what I said. Now if you'll excuse me, the front doorbell's ringing."

"Wait!" Lisa begged. "Which hospital? Where?"

"Mt. Sinai in Boston," the housekeeper said. "Would you like to leave your name and number so I can give him a message when he comes home?"

68

As Lisa frantically scribbled the name of the hospital onto a piece of paper, the phone slipped from her hand and she dropped the receiver. It swung free on its cord and hit the wall with a loud bang. She grabbed it back and started to talk again. "Uh . . . yes, I'll leave my name," she stammered. "I mean, no, no, I guess I don't really want to after all. That is . . . can you tell me what's wrong with Rob anyway? What does he have?"

All at once, she realized the voice on the other end of the line was gone, and she was listening to a loud dial tone. The housekeeper had hung up the phone before Lisa could learn just how sick Rob really was.

CHAPTER TEN

Lisa rushed back to the suite, flung open the door, and leaned against the wall. She was so upset she couldn't say a word.

The other girls saw her white face and hurried over.

"Lisa!" Shanon cried. "Are you all right? Did you get to talk to Rob or not?"

Lisa shook her head and tears ran down her cheeks.

"What happened?" Amy asked. "Come inside and tell us what's wrong!"

"It's Rob," Lisa whispered through her tears. "He . . . he's . . . not home after all."

"Where is he?" Palmer asked.

"In the hospital!"

Amy and Shanon gasped, and Palmer let out a long breath. "Oh no!" she said. "That's terrible! What happened to him? Was he in an accident?"

Lisa shook her head. "I don't know. I only talked to the housekeeper, and I dropped the phone, and she hung up before I could find out what was wrong."

She moved away from the wall and sank into the nearest chair. "I don't think it could have been an accident, though. I mean, Rob wrote me he was going to be busy, so he must have known he was going into the hospital."

"So, unless he was in an accident on his way home," Amy reasoned, "that must mean he's sick."

"Right," Lisa said. She gave a long, shuddering sigh. "And I have a terrible feeling it must be something really bad. That's probably why he didn't tell me where he was going!"

The girls all felt anxious and worried, but everyone was surprised when Palmer suddenly burst into tears. "Simmie must have known Rob was so sick he was going into the hospital. But he still went ahead with those mean tricks. And all the while he was trying to embarrass him, Rob was probably lying on an operating table with tubes stuck up his nose! He didn't tell me that part. He really didn't."

Amy went over and patted Palmer on the back. "Calm down, Palmer," she said soothingly. "If you didn't know Rob was sick, you can't blame yourself for that part."

Palmer put her face in her hands and broke into fresh sobs. When she finally looked up, her tear-streaked face was stormy. "You're right," she said. "I can't blame myself

71

for not knowing Rob was sick. But I can blame Simmie. He had to have known. I'm going to write him a letter right now and tell him how I feel about that!"

Dear Simmie,

How could you do this to me? You told me we were tricking Rob to embarrass him, but you didn't tell me he was really sick! Now all my roommates hate me, and I'm the one who's embarrassed!

Thanks for nothing,
Palmer

Meanwhile, Amy, Shanon, and Lisa were talking in Lisa and Shanon's bedroom. "I wish we knew what was wrong with Rob," Amy said. "Do you think you could call that housekeeper back and ask her?"

"I don't think so," Lisa said. "She didn't seem very thrilled to be talking to me in the first place. And I might get Rob in trouble with his parents if I keep calling him all the time."

"I have another idea," Shanon said. "Amy and I can write to Mars and John and see if they know what's wrong with Rob. They're his suitemates, after all. He must have told them why he was going into the hospital."

"That's a good idea," Lisa said. "But it will take a while for your letters to get there, and for the answers to get back. I'll go crazy before that!"

"I know!" Amy said excitedly. "We can send a communication from the *Ledger* office computer to the Ardsley Lit. Mag. computer like we did last winter. That won't take any time at all!"

"I don't think that's a very good idea," Lisa said. "My brother told me that the headmaster at Ardsley just caught a bunch of the guys over there using that computer to send some *really* personal messages to their girlfriends back home. We'd better lay off it—at least for a while."

Lisa started pacing the floor, trying to figure out what to do. All at once, she skidded to a stop. "I just thought of something really awful!" she cried. "I sent that nasty letter to Rob at Ardsley. What if the school forwards it to the hospital? What if he's lying there in bed, waiting to go into surgery, and a nurse hands him that letter? He might have a heart attack or something!"

Lisa sounded as if she were going to start crying again, and Shanon spoke up quickly. "Didn't you say that the Williams' housekeeper told you which hospital Rob was in?" she asked.

"Yes she did. It's Mt. Sinai in Boston."

"Well, then, why don't you write Rob another letter and mail it to the hospital? If you send it special delivery, he'll probably get it by tomorrow."

Lisa went over to Shanon and gave her a hug. "Thanks, Shanon," she said. "That's exactly what I'll do. If I'm lucky, the nice letter will get there before the mean one!"

While Lisa sat down at her desk, Amy and Shanon got out their pens and stationery and wrote to their own pen pals.

Dear John,
   You sure have some totally weird stuff going on over there at Ard-Barf. What's the word on your roomie Rob? We heard he was in the hospital! Please let us know what's wrong with him. We are desperate!
                                                    Hungry for knowledge,
                                                    Amy

Dear Mars,
   I know I owe you a letter about myself, but this time I'm really writing for Lisa. She found out Rob was in the hospital, but she didn't find out what's wrong with him, and she's really going crazy. Could you please write back soon and let us know—if you know, that is? Thanks a lot, and I hope you're not sick!
                                                    Your pen pal,
                                                    Shanon

   Lisa stared out the window for a few minutes, chewing on her pen and trying to figure out what she wanted to say to Rob. She wrote a few sentences, but then crumpled up the page and threw it away. She made several more false starts with no success. Finally, she told herself to be

74

completely honest and say whatever came into her mind. Soon she relaxed, and the words came pouring out onto the paper.

Dear Rob,

I have so many things to say to you, I don't know where to start. First of all, I found out you're in the hospital— well, you probably already figured out I know because I'm sending this letter there! I'm really sorry that you're sick . . . or hurt, or whatever you are, and I wish you'd told me about it before. If you weren't sick, I'd be mad at you for not trusting me enough to tell me. But anyway, I hope it's nothing too bad. I'd feel terrible if anything happened to you. (I didn't know how terrible until I heard where you were!)

The other thing I have to do is explain something to you. I hope you haven't gotten a really nasty letter from me already, but if you have, I DIDN'T MEAN IT! If you haven't, DON'T READ IT! Don't even open it. TEAR IT UP! There's a long story behind it that I'll tell you someday when you're better. I just want you to know that I don't hate you. I don't have any bad feelings for you at all. But I do have a lot of really good feelings. I wish you were here instead of in the hospital so I could tell you about them. For now, I'll just say I think you're terrific, and leave it at that.

I know you're probably not up to it right now, but

getting a letter from you would be about the nicest thing in the world that could happen to me right now. You wouldn't believe what's been going on around here!

Please get better fast and take good care of yourself.

Love,
Lisa

CHAPTER ELEVEN

Late that night, Lisa lay wide awake on her bed, staring up at the ceiling. The sound of Shanon's soft breathing from across the room told Lisa that her roommate was sound asleep. But sleep was impossible for Lisa. She'd been trying for hours, twisting and turning in her hot, sweaty sheets. She'd counted sheep, done yoga, and tried counting backwards from one hundred to one, but nothing had worked.

All she could do was think about Rob, lying in the hospital, surrounded by doctors and nurses. If only she knew what was wrong with him! Maybe he *had* been in a terrible accident on his way home for a visit. Maybe he had a mysterious disease, and no one knew what it was. Maybe he was dying! His last words might be for Lisa—and no one in his family even knew who she was!

This last thought made Lisa break out in a cold sweat. She sat bolt upright in her bed. She was sure she was right.

Even though she and Rob had been pen pals since last fall, she'd never told her parents about it, and she was positive Rob wouldn't have told his family either. Something awful could happen to him, and she might not find out for a long time. His parents might not even let his suitemates know. Why would they? If something happened to Lisa, *her* parents wouldn't call her roommates. They'd be too upset.

Suddenly, Lisa's mind started whirling at top speed. She knew what she had to do. She *had* to see Rob in the hospital, and she knew just how to do it. She could ride her bike into town right now and take the late night bus to Boston. She wasn't sure where Mt. Sinai Hospital was, but someone at the bus station in Boston would tell her, or else she'd take a taxi. Then, when she got to the hospital, she could pretend to be Rob's sister so they'd let her go up to his room. She'd only have to visit him for a few minutes to make sure he was okay. After that, she'd take the return bus and be back at school by tomorrow afternoon.

By the time she'd put on a pair of soft, faded jeans and a huge baggy Harvard sweatshirt, she'd already thought of several problems with her plan. For one thing, she'd miss her morning classes. As she sat down on the edge of the bed to pull on her favorite purple leg warmers, she glanced over at Shanon. She could, she supposed, wake her roommate and ask her to make excuses for her the next day.

She tiptoed toward Shanon's bed but then changed her mind. For one thing, the other girl was sleeping so peacefully it would be a shame to wake her up. But more

78

importantly, it didn't seem fair to ask Shanon to lie for her. Shanon was so totally honest—she blushed at the very idea of telling a lie. Besides, if Lisa got caught leaving the campus at night without permission, she could easily be expelled from school. She knew Shanon would help if she asked her to, but it just wasn't right to involve her in such a risky plan.

Lisa tiptoed out of the bedroom and into the sitting room, where she started rummaging around, looking for her backpack. All at once, a voice whispered to her out of the darkness.

"Lisa, is that you?"

Lisa was so surprised she jumped and stubbed her toe against the leg of the sofa. "Ow!" She grabbed her foot and hopped around. Then she sat down to rub her toe. "Palmer?" she asked, peering into the corner. Her heart started to thump inside her chest. What in the world was Palmer doing up at this time of night?

"Yes, it's me." A shadowy figure in a white nightgown rose up from a chair and came over to the sofa. Lisa couldn't see her face, but from the husky, cracked sound of her voice, she could tell Palmer had been crying.

"What are you doing up so late, Palmer?" she asked.

"Oh, I don't know," Palmer sighed. "I just couldn't sleep."

"Me either," Lisa said. "What's the matter with you?"

"I feel terrible about everything," Palmer answered. "I'm sorry Rob's sick, and I'm sorry I went along with

Simmie's rotten tricks . . . and I'm really sorry you and Shanon and Amy all hate me."

Lisa was quiet for a minute. "Palmer," she said at last, "I am very very angry with you—or at least I *was*. But I don't hate you."

"Thanks," Palmer said hoarsely. "I know I only think about myself and what I want to do. But that's all going to change, I promise. From now on, I'll be kind and considerate and generous and . . . and . . . perfect!"

Lisa smiled at her suitemate through the darkness. "Well, you don't have to be *that* good," she said. "You'll make everybody sick."

Palmer laughed and blew her nose on a tissue. "I'm just glad you don't hate me after what I did," she said.

"How could I hate you, Palmer?" Lisa said. "The Foxes can get mad at each other, but they never *hate* each other!" She crouched down on her hands and knees to feel around on the floor for her backpack. "Aha!" she said, pulling it out from under the sofa and standing up again.

It was only then that Palmer noticed Lisa was completely dressed. "Hey!" she exclaimed. "Why do you have your clothes on in the middle of the night? Are you going someplace?"

Lisa didn't say anything for a minute. Even though Palmer had apologized, Lisa still wasn't sure she could be trusted.

But on the other hand, Lisa thought, Palmer *had* been up crying just now and she *had* sounded really sorry about all the trouble she'd caused. Lisa decided she might as well go ahead and tell her. What harm could it do. Palmer already knew she was going *somewhere*. Besides, it might be a good idea to have a friend who knew where she was heading.

"I'm going to Boston," Lisa explained in a whisper. "To see Rob in the hospital."

Palmer sucked in her breath in surprise. "How are you getting there?" she asked. "You can't ride your bike that far!"

"I'll ride it into town. Then I'll take the bus to Boston."

"I don't know, Lisa. Couldn't you wait until tomorrow? This sounds dangerous. I mean, I've never actually been to the Boston bus station, but the ones I've seen in Florida are the pits in broad daylight. And now it's the middle of the night!"

"That's why it's the perfect time for me to go," Lisa explained. "It's dark now, and no one will see me. If I wait till tomorrow, I'll never get away with it." She finally found her wallet, buried in the front pocket of her backpack. "Let's see. Ten, eleven, twelve dollars. I guess that'll be enough for the bus. I wish I hadn't blown all that allowance money on pizza last week."

As Lisa put on her backpack and started toward the door, Palmer put a hand on her arm. "Don't go," she pleaded. "Please wait till tomorrow. Maybe then you could call Rob's house again, or . . ."

Lisa wheeled around. "You don't understand," she said

81

fiercely. "I *can't* wait! I have to find out what's wrong with Rob *now!*"

"Okay then," Palmer said. "If you have to go, go. But let me give you some more money. If you got into some kind of trouble . . . well, twelve dollars might not be enough." She hurried into her bedroom and came out with her soft little leather coin purse. She took out two bills and pressed them into Lisa's hand.

Lisa went over to the window and peered at the bills in the dim moonlight. "Palmer, these are twenty-dollar bills! You can't give me forty dollars!"

"You'll pay me back later," Palmer said. "Besides, I can afford it."

"I know you can, but—"

"If you're really going through with this," Palmer interrupted, "shouldn't you go? You don't want to miss the bus!"

Lisa came away from the window and gave the other girl a big hug. "Thanks, Palmer," she whispered.

Palmer hugged her back. "Just be careful," she said. "I'll cover for you tomorrow if anyone asks where you are."

"Thanks," Lisa said again. She stepped out into the hall, but Palmer followed her.

"Here," she said. "Here's the key to my bike lock. Take my bicycle. It's faster than yours."

"Thanks, Palmer," Lisa said for the third time. "I'll be careful with it. 'Bye!"

Before Palmer could think of anything else to give her, Lisa ran down the hall to the stairway that led down to the basement bike room. When she reached the basement, it was so dark and spooky, she could hardly see where she was going. She wished she could turn on a light, but she didn't dare risk it. Somebody outside might see it and think she was a thief.

She fumbled along the dark hallway, opened the door to the bike storage room, and immediately realized she would *have* to turn on a light. The room had only one small window to the outside, and it was almost completely black inside. There was no way she'd be able to find Palmer's or anyone else's bike in this darkness.

Well, she'd just have to risk it. If she moved fast, the light would only be on for a few seconds. Besides, it wasn't very likely that anyone would be walking around outside at this late hour.

Lisa snapped on the light and ran to the far rack where Palmer's beautiful silver bike was kept. She pulled out the tiny key, opened the padlock, and took the bike out of the rack. Then she hurried back to the light switch and snapped it off. She was wheeling the bike out of the storage room when she heard the low rumble of a man's voice coming from the end of the hall.

Lisa froze for a few seconds. Then, as silently as possible, she tried to reverse her steps and pull the bike back into the bike room. The front wheel swung to the side and banged into the doorframe.

Just then, a flashlight beam hit her right between the eyes. "Lisa!" a shocked voice exclaimed. The overhead light came on, and Lisa blinked. Then she swallowed hard. Dan Griffith and Maggie Grayson were standing at the end of the hallway staring right at her.

CHAPTER TWELVE

Lisa felt hot and cold all at the same time. She stared at the two teachers and started to say something, but no words came out of her mouth. Frantically, she tried to think of an excuse. If she could come up with some innocent explanation for why she was down in the bike room at one o'clock in the morning, she might be able to get away with this after all. But what could she possibly say? Her clothes, backpack, and bike told the whole story. She was running away from school in the middle of the night! It was just about the worst crime a student at Alma Stephens could commit.

Lisa knew what Miss Grayson was supposed to do in a situation like this. She was supposed to go right to Miss Pryn and wake her up. Then Miss Pryn would call Lisa's parents, and they'd have to come to the school for a big conference about Lisa's punishment. It would be a big horrendous deal. It might even end up with Lisa being suspended or kicked out of school!

But, horrible as that would be, it wasn't what was worrying Lisa at the moment. All she cared about now was Rob. She *had* to go see him in the hospital. She *had* to find out what was wrong with him!

"Miss Grayson," she said, when she could finally find her voice. "Please, *please* go away and pretend you didn't see me here. There's something I have to do . . . someplace I have to go. If you stop me now . . . I won't be able to stand it! I'll go crazy!"

Her voice echoed off the basement walls. Even to Lisa's own ears, her words sounded hysterical. All at once, she knew Miss Grayson would never let her go, and she broke down into loud, gasping sobs.

Miss Grayson and Mr. Griffith exchanged a long look. "I think I can take this from here, Dan," Miss Grayson said quietly. "Thank you for a lovely evening."

Mr. Griffith just smiled at Miss Grayson and said good night. But as he was going up the stairs, he looked and gave Lisa a wink over his shoulder. She didn't know exactly what it meant, but it did make her feel a little better. She swallowed hard and tried to stop crying.

Miss Grayson walked down the hall and put a hand on Lisa's heaving back. "Calm down, sweetie," she said. "Whatever it is, it can't be that bad."

"But it . . . it *is*," Lisa managed to gasp. "It's terrible!"

Miss Grayson squeezed her shoulder. "All right then,"

she said. "It's terrible. But we can still talk about it. Why don't you put the bike away so we can go to my apartment and figure out what to do about . . . whatever it is that's upsetting you so much."

Lisa nodded dumbly and wheeled Palmer's bike back to its place on the rack. Then she let Miss Grayson lead her to her cheerful little sitting room.

"I'll make some chamomile tea," the French teacher said, reaching for a delicate china teapot. "I've heard it's supposed to have a soothing effect."

Lisa sank into a soft easy chair and watched Miss Grayson putter around the room, measuring tea into the pot, boiling water on her hot plate, and getting out two dainty blue and white teacups and a matching plate of chocolate shortbread cookies. She knew nothing had happened to change her situation, but for some reason she already felt a little better about everything. First of all, Miss Grayson wasn't acting as if she were about to turn her in to Miss Pryn. And, though it didn't seem possible, maybe she'd even be able to help Lisa figure out what to do about Rob.

"Do you like milk and sugar in your tea?" Miss Grayson asked her.

Lisa nodded and tried to smile.

"Okay," Miss Grayson answered, handing her a steaming cup. "Now, why don't you have a cookie. Then start at the beginning and tell me the whole story."

Lisa took a small sip of the tea and put her cup down on

Miss Grayson's coffee table. "It's . . . it's about Rob Williams," she began haltingly. "You know, my pen pal from Ardsley?"

Miss Grayson nodded and bit into one of the cookies. "The whole dorm knows about the Foxes' pen pals—The Great Unknown," she teased. "Go on."

Lisa told the teacher the whole story. When she got to the part about how she'd written Rob the nasty letter and then discovered he was sick, she dissolved into tears once again.

Miss Grayson handed her a tissue. "And now you're worried that he'll get the letter and think you're really angry with him?" she asked sympathetically.

Lisa nodded through her tears. "It's more than just that," she sobbed. "You see, I don't even know *why* he's in the hospital. I don't have the slightest idea what's wrong with him. I didn't know how to find out, either. So I decided to go into Boston tonight and ask him myself."

Miss Grayson's eyes widened with surprise. "You mean *that's* where you were going tonight? You were going to ride Palmer's bike all the way to Boston?"

Lisa shook her head. "Just into town," she said, "to take the late-night bus." She wiped her eyes and asked for another tissue.

Miss Grayson handed her the whole box. "You must really care about Rob, Lisa. To take a risk like that, I mean."

Lisa nodded again. "I guess I really do care about him—a lot."

Miss Grayson thought for a minute. "Do you know which hospital your friend is in?" she asked.

"The Williams' housekeeper told me. He's in Mt. Sinai."

Miss Grayson clapped her hands together and smiled. "We're in luck then," she cried. "I have a friend who works there."

She jumped to her feet, picked up the phone on her desk, and dialed the number. "Would you please page Dr. Sarah Lyon?" she said into the phone. "She's a resident in pediatrics. My name is Maggie Grayson." She sat down on the desk and winked at Lisa. "They put me on hold," she whispered.

"Hi, Sarah!" she said a few minutes later. "Sorry to bother you at this hour, but I knew you'd be there. We have a small crisis here at Stephens, and I wonder if you could help me out. Do you happen to know the status of a patient named Rob . . . Williams, is it, Lisa?"

Lisa nodded and gripped the arms of her chair. Miss Grayson said, "Of course, I'll wait," into the phone and rolled her eyes at Lisa. She covered the mouthpiece with her hand. "I'm on hold again," she explained. "Sarah's looking up Rob's chart."

Lisa dug her nails into the upholstery. She wanted to know what was wrong with Rob, but suddenly she was scared stiff about finding out. If only Miss Grayson's friend would hurry up!

"Hi, Sarah!" Miss Grayson was saying. "Oh. Oh really? Uh-huh. Tomorrow you say? Well thank you very much. Yes, we'll get together for dinner soon. Who? Oh, yes, he's fine. . . . In fact, he's terrific. Yes, I'll call you soon. Thanks again."

By the time Miss Grayson had finished chatting with her friend, Lisa felt ready to faint. The instant the teacher hung up, Lisa jumped to her feet. "What did the doctor say?" she asked. "Is Rob all right?"

Miss Grayson smiled and gave her a little hug. "Well, it sounds good to me," she laughed. "In fact, he's going home tomorrow. He's being discharged."

Lisa's mouth dropped open. "Going home tomorrow?" she repeated. "How can that be?" She had a terrible thought. "Does that mean there's nothing more they can do for him? It's . . . hopeless?"

"I guess it's hopeless to keep him there when he's already had his tonsils out!"

Lisa gasped and sank back down into her chair. "Tonsils," she breathed. "He was only having his tonsils out? And I thought . . . Why that's no big deal at all! I had my tonsils out when I was seven. I had a sore throat for a while, but my father bought me all the chocolate chocolate-chip ice cream I could eat after that! It was great!"

She giggled and jumped back up on her feet. She hugged Miss Grayson again and started dancing around the room. "Oh, Mag . . . er, Miss Grayson," she said, "if you only knew what I've been through. I was so worried. I couldn't figure out why he didn't tell me where he was going, and I thought he might have been in an accident, or have some terrible disease, and you wouldn't believe how crazy I got."

"I *would* believe it," Miss Grayson smiled at her. "I've just watched you go from being hysterically upset to hysterically happy in one minute, remember? Rob must be a pretty terrific boy."

"Oh he *is*," Lisa agreed enthusiastically. "He's smart and funny and cute and sweet. But you know what's the most amazing thing about this whole mess? It's what I learned about myself. I mean, I knew all those good things about Rob before, but I didn't really appreciate them until I heard he was in the hospital! I knew I liked him, but I didn't know how much till I thought I might never see him again. Isn't that absolutely insane?"

Miss Grayson patted her on the shoulder. "I don't think it's insane at all," she said. "It happens to people all the time. You know you like someone, but you don't realize just how much until you think you might lose him or her. The important thing is to *remember* and appreciate those feelings even when the person is healthy again."

Lisa sighed. "I will!"

Miss Grayson glanced at her watch and her eyes grew wide. "Look how late it is!" she exclaimed. "I have to get you to bed right away." She glanced at Lisa's excited face. "Though I don't suppose you'll get much sleep tonight."

Lisa shook her head and laughed. "No, I won't," she

said. "I'm too up in the air. I'll probably fall asleep tomorrow, right in the middle of French class."

Miss Grayson laughed, too. "Well, I'll excuse it tomorrow under the circumstances," she said. Then her face grew grave. "But there's something else I can't excuse, young lady."

Abruptly, Lisa stopped smiling. She knew she deserved a lecture, but she'd been hoping to get away without one.

"What you were planning to do tonight was foolhardy to say the least," Miss Grayson began. "A young girl going to a big city bus station in the middle of the night!" She shook her head. "You are too intelligent a person not to know that's dangerous, and just plain stupid, Lisa!"

Lisa nodded. "I know," she said in a small voice. "I just didn't think about the danger. All I could think about was Rob."

"I know that, sweetie. But all you had to do was ask somebody for help. You could have gone to Kate Majors, for instance. That's why we put upperclassmen on the freshmen halls."

Lisa snickered and rolled her eyes, and Miss Grayson smiled. "Well, I guess Kate can be a little offputting at times," she said diplomatically. "But I can assure you she has a good heart. If you went to her with a real problem, I know she'd help you."

"I guess so," Lisa muttered. She still knew Kate Majors was the last person in the world she'd go to with a problem.

92

"And then there's me," Miss Grayson went on. "I'm always ready to listen, and I love giving advice. Sometimes I can even help you figure out what to do!"

"You sure did tonight," Lisa told her gratefully. "You saved my life!"

Miss Grayson laughed. "Well, I don't know about that," she said. "But I do know I want you to promise me you'll never do anything so crazy again!"

"I won't, Miss Grayson," Lisa said solemnly. "Believe me, I won't!"

"I do believe you, Lisa. But, as a faculty member, I also believe I can't let you off with just a lecture for something this serious." Miss Grayson chewed on her lip for a few seconds. "I just can't seem to think of the appropriate disciplinary action. Any ideas?"

"I could help Mrs. Butter with breakfast preparation in the kitchen every morning before breakfast for a week!" Lisa volunteered. "I'd *hate* that—particularly if she made me help dish out that slimy disgusting kippered herring she's always giving us!"

"Make that two weeks of breakfast preparation, and we've got a deal," Miss Grayson said. "I'll talk to Mrs. Butter first thing tomorrow morning and make sure she knows you'll be coming the next day. I'm going to tell her you'll be reporting for kippered-herring duty at five forty-five every morning. And she's not to accept any excuses!"

Lisa groaned. "Five forty-five *a.m.*?" she asked.

"That's when Mrs. Butter gets there," Miss Grayson

pointed out. "Of course, if you think it's too early and you'd rather have Miss Pryn suggest a suitable punishment . . ."

"No!" Lisa exclaimed. "I'll be in the kitchen at five forty-five on the dot every day for two weeks. I promise!"

"All right then," Miss Grayson told her. "And now that that's settled, get yourself off to bed so we can both get some sleep!"

Lisa gave her teacher one last hug. Then she scampered off down the hall toward her room. She wished tomorrow would hurry up and come. She could hardly wait to tell her roommates what they'd missed during the night!

CHAPTER THIRTEEN

———◆———

Dear Palmer,

I'm sorry my little tricks made your roomates lose their cool. Yes, I did know Rob was going into the hospital, but he asked us not to tell anyone because he was embarassed about having a baby operation like having his tonsels out. I guess I should have embarassed him by telling everyone about that *instead of tricking Lisa!*

> Hoping you're not still angry with me,
> Simmie

P.S. I haven't heard from the Hydraulic Dudes yet, but they say I only have one more stunt left to perform and I'm in for sure. Anyway, I know they'll accept me when they see the new pair of Polo sunglasses I just got.

Dear Amy,

The word on the grapevine is that Lisa already knows Rob was just having a minor gig at the hospital. Yours truly told *him* to tell *her* where he was going, but would he listen? No way!

Now you can fill me in on something. Someone here got hold of an Alma Stephens newspaper in which there's an article about a co-ed Strawberry Pancake Breakfast you're planning over there. I love strawberries! I love pancakes! I love co-eds! This is a hint!

> Write back soon,
> Your pen pal, John

Dear Shanon,

"The course of true love never did run smooth." (Do you like the play this is from? I do!) But I guess you've heard that Rob and Lisa smoothed *things out in this case* anyway, and that Rob was only having his tonsils out in the hospital, so, as our mutual friend the bard said, "All's Well That Ends Well."

My roommate John just showed me an interesting article in a smuggled copy of the Stephens newspaper that was being passed around over here. Very *interesting. Did you* write it?

> Yours in poetry,
> Mars

When Amy, Shanon, and Palmer finished reading their pen pals' letters out loud, they all looked up and giggled.

"Wow," Amy said, "John and Mars are really hinting around about the Strawberry Pancake Breakfast. I guess

96

we'll just have to write back and invite them to be our dates!"

"We have no choice." Shanon smiled. "I wonder if I could write my invitation in the form of a sonnet. I think Mars would really appreciate it. I'm going to start right now." She got to her feet and went to the desk for a pen and some paper.

"I'm going to write John right away, too," Amy said. "Just as soon as I finish packing up that Elvis poster for Evon in Australia. What about you, Palmer? Are you going to invite Simmie?"

Palmer looked thoughtful. "Well, I don't know," she said. "He didn't mention it in his letter the way your pen pals did. But he *did* apologize about the dirty tricks and everything. . . ."

"Which you knew about before they happened, don't forget," Amy reminded her.

"Just one of them," Palmer said.

"Come on, you two," Shanon called from the desk. "Don't you remember we agreed not to talk about that stuff anymore? Everyone has apologized, so it's time we put it all behind us!"

"Right," Amy agreed. "Sorry, Palmer. What were you going to say about Simmie?"

"Oh, I guess I'll just go ahead and invite him. After all, he is just about the best-looking boy in the world. And I'd die for a chance to see him in a pair of Polo sunglasses!"

"That's settled then," Shanon said. She carried over pens

and stationery for Palmer and Amy, and the three girls settled down to write their letters. Just then, Lisa came through the door. She had just finished with crew practice and was looking flushed and windblown.

"Oh!" she exclaimed when she saw what they were doing. "You all got letters!"

"Right," Amy told her. "We're all writing back to ask The Unknown to the Strawberry Pancake Breakfast."

"What's that?" Lisa asked.

"I can't believe you haven't heard about it!" Amy said.

"The seniors are putting it on," Shanon explained. "They actually go into the kitchen and cook strawberry pancakes for the whole school."

"Ugh!" Palmer said. "I didn't know the seniors were cooking the breakfast. We'll probably all get food poisoning!"

"Well, it's a yearly tradition," Shanon said, "and I haven't heard of anyone dying from it before."

"It's also a yearly tradition that Ardsley's invited to the breakfast!" Amy said happily. "And both Mars and John are hinting around that they want to be our dates."

"I'm inviting Simmie, too," Palmer said, "even though he didn't drop any hints. I don't want to be the only Fox without a date for the breakfast!"

"*I* might be the one without a date," Lisa said. "I wonder how long it will take Rob to recuperate."

"Don't worry," Amy said. "The breakfast's not for two

weeks. He should be back at school before then, shouldn't he?"

"I think so," Lisa said. "I wish I could find out for sure."

"Well, why don't you call him up at home and ask?" Amy suggested. "You know he's not in the hospital anymore, so he has to be there."

"You're right," Lisa said decisively. "I'm going to do just that! Now if I can just find enough change for the pay phone. . . ."

Without saying a word, Shanon, Amy, and Palmer all reached for their purses and handed Lisa all their nickels, dimes, and quarters. "I must owe you a hundred dollars by now with all this change I'm borrowing!" Lisa laughed. "I promise I'll pay you guys back!"

Lisa left the room and headed for the phone at the end of the hall. This time, she knew just how much money to put into the coin slots. The phone rang twice before the housekeeper picked it up.

"Williams residence."

"May I speak to Rob Williams please?"

"One moment. I'll see if he's resting."

A few minutes later, a scratchy voice spoke into the phone. "Hello?"

"Rob? It's me. Lisa. I hope it's okay that I'm calling you at home."

"Hey! Lisa. Sure it's okay. I mean that you're calling. I was just lying here thinking about you."

Lisa's heart did a little flip-flop in her chest, but she tried to make her voice sound normal. "You sound like a frog. Does it hurt when you talk?"

"Well, a little I guess. The doctor told me I could only talk for a few minutes at a time. But that doesn't mean I want you to hang up!"

"I'll do most of the talking then," Lisa promised. "But first you have to tell me if you're okay."

"Yeah, I'm okay," Rob said. "My throat's pretty sore, but they're letting me eat orange sherbet for breakfast, lunch, and dinner, so it's not so bad. I'll look like a blimp when I get back to school, though. You won't want anything to do with me!"

Lisa giggled. Then she cleared her throat. "Did you tear up that awful letter I sent you?"

Rob was quiet for a minute. "You want me to tear it up?" he asked. "How come? Didn't you mean what you said?"

"No!" Lisa nearly shouted. "I didn't mean a word of it. I thought I wrote you that!"

"Oh," Rob said. "I'm sorry to hear that. I was hoping you meant all that stuff."

Lisa frowned at her end of the phone. Rob had *wanted* her to say she hated him? Somehow, this conversation wasn't making any sense! All at once, the explanation came to her. "Wait a minute," she said. "Are we talking about the same letter?"

"I don't know," Rob croaked. "I'm talking about the letter I got at the hospital right before I left. I didn't think it was awful at all. I thought it was fantastic. But now that you're telling me to tear it up . . ."

Lisa felt her cheeks becoming bright red. She let out a long breath. "I didn't mean *that* letter," she said in a small voice. "I meant the letter I sent you at school. The one I told you about in the hospital letter."

"Oh *that* letter," Rob said. "I haven't gotten any of my mail from school yet so I haven't read it. Now that you mention it, I do remember that you wrote something in the hospital letter about tearing up a nasty letter. But I guess I wasn't paying attention to that part. I was too busy reading the other parts . . . about a million times."

"Oh," Lisa said. Her heart thumped again. Just then the operator came on the line. "Please deposit fifty cents to continue this conversation."

Lisa dropped in her last two quarters. Then she spoke all in a rush. "I'll hurry up now because I know I should let you go so you can rest your voice, but I have one more question. Would you like to go to the Alma Stephens Pancake Breakfast with me? It's in two weeks."

"I'd like that," Rob said in his hoarse voice. "A lot."

"Okay," Lisa said breathlessly. "I'll see you then!"

Rob said good-bye and Lisa hung up the phone. Then she leaned back against the wall, closed her eyes, and grinned. She couldn't believe how well everything was

101

turning out, especially after the disaster with Simmie and the tricks and the sweater and the nasty letter. It was just like that corny thing her grandmother always said. "It's always darkest before the dawn." Lisa had never believed it before. But in this case, Grammy knew *exactly* what she was talking about!

CHAPTER FOURTEEN

Dear Mars,
    Shall I invite thee
    To a pancake day?
    Thou wilt eat cakes and have some berries, too.
    Seniors will cook them
    In a wondrous way,
    And we will share that bounty, me and you.
    The breakfast takes place
    On the tenth of May,
    The Ardsley bus will bring thee here at nine.
    Please join me, Mars,
    On Pancake Saturday,
    'T would be a joy
    If by my side you'd dine.

                                    Thy pen pal,
                                    Shanon

Dear John,

I love pancakes, too—all those carbs are good for a healthy bod. I hope you'll bring your bod on the bus on Saturday, May 10th, at 9:00 for the Strawberry Pancake Breakfast (that you just happened to mention in your letter)! I'm going to run two miles before you come, so I can stuff myself. Please bring yourself and your appetite!

Amy

Dear Simmie,

Guess what? This is your lucky day. I accept your apology! Now I want to invite you to be my date for the Strawberry Pancake Breakfast on the 10th. Please let me know what you'll be wearing so I can coordinate my outfit. See you Saturday!

Palmer

P.S. Don't forget your sunglasses.

Lisa was the only one of the Foxes who didn't write a letter inviting her pen pal to the Pancake Breakfast. She'd already invited hers on the phone. It had been an incredible conversation, she thought. No matter what she did, she couldn't stop going over every single word Rob had said to her. Sometimes thinking about the conversation made her feel excited and happy. Other times, it made her feel embarrassed, shy, and jumpy. If only she could be sure that it was all for real.

CHAPTER FIFTEEN

The day of the Pancake Breakfast was warm and sunny. All four Foxes were up early, washing and drying their hair and picking out their outfits. Because it was a Saturday and a special occasion, they didn't have to wear regulation Alma Stephens clothes. They were allowed to choose anything they wanted—"at their own discretion, but within reason," Miss Pryn had put it in her Friday morning announcement.

By 8:30, three of the suitemates were dressed. Amy was wearing a shiny black jumpsuit with a metallic belt, while Palmer had on a pale blue tailored cotton dress and sweater that matched her eyes perfectly. Shanon had borrowed some long, oversized Hawaiian-print shorts and a bright red sleeveless T-shirt from Lisa. But Lisa herself was still running around in her nightgown.

"Come *on*, Lisa!" Palmer said impatiently. "Get dressed!"

Lisa looked at the pile of discarded outfits on her bed. "I don't have anything to wear," she complained.

"You probably wanted to wear these things," Shanon said worriedly, looking down at her borrowed clothes. "I'll take them off and find something else to put on."

She started to pull off the Hawaiian shorts, but Lisa stopped her. "No, no, no," she said. "Don't take those off! That outfit looks much better on you than it does on me anyway." She pawed through her clothes again. "I just can't make up my mind, that's all."

Palmer snorted in disgust. "If you don't hurry up," she said, "we won't be able to get a table together, and Simmie and I will have to sit with Kate Majors or some other dweeb like that."

She eyed Lisa thoughtfully. Then she went into her own bedroom and came back with a silky knee-length scarlet shirt and a pair of snug-fitting white leggings. "Why don't you wear these, Lisa?" she suggested. "They were a birthday present from my aunt. I've never even worn them, but they look like the type of far-out thing you like."

"Palmer," Lisa breathed. "They're perfect. Really radical, but nice too. But I can't borrow something you've never even worn before!"

"To tell you the truth, I probably never will wear them—so you might as well. It just kills me that my aunt would send me something bright red like this. With my fair

106

coloring, red makes me look all washed out and sickly. But on you, with all that dark hair, it wouldn't look too bad."

Lisa jumped up and gave Palmer a quick hug. "Thanks a million," she said excitedly. "I know I won't be nervous at all in this outfit. It will give me extra confidence."

She put on the clothes and dug out a pair of soft red leather ballet slippers that were an exact match for the shirt. Then she ran a brush over her long hair. With one final glance in the sitting-room mirror, the four girls hurried outside to meet the Ardsley bus.

Because the day was so warm, the Pancake Breakfast was being served on the front lawn. Long folding tables and chairs had been set up on the grass. The tables were decorated with brightly colored paper tablecloths and jars full of daisies and carnations. Senior girls were running back and forth, setting out containers of syrup and butter on each of the tables.

The Ardsley bus was just pulling into the driveway as the group walked out of Fox Hall. Shanon, Amy, and Palmer hurried forward with a crowd of other girls, eager to see the boys. But Lisa hung back. Even though she'd said she wouldn't be nervous in Palmer's outfit, she was suddenly overcome with shyness. She wondered if Rob was feeling the same way.

A few minutes later, Reggie got off the bus and waved to her. She waved back. Then she stood on tiptoe to watch as boy after boy climbed down from the bus. Finally, the door closed and the bus drove away. Rob hadn't come!

107

Lisa couldn't believe this was happening to her—again! She'd been so sure that everything would work out this time. As Lisa's eyes filled with tears, she suddenly heard Amy's voice in her ear. "What do you suppose happened to them?"

"You mean John wasn't on the bus either?" Lisa asked.

"Or Mars or Simmie!" Shanon cried as she and Palmer came up to join them. "All four of The Unknown are missing!"

Just then, the girls heard the loud chug-a-chug of a motor. They turned around just as a creaky, dilapidated old farm truck pulled into the driveway. The back of the truck was filled with crates of squawking, clucking chickens.

"What on earth is that disgusting smelly truck doing here?" Palmer asked. "Did it make a wrong turn or what?"

The truck groaned and clanked to a stop. Then the driver climbed down from his seat and went around to open the back. As the rear gate opened, four boys climbed down from among the cages. The girls recognized Rob, Mars, and John at once. "But who's that dark-haired boy in the funny clothes?" Palmer asked. "And where's Simmie?"

John saw where they were standing and came over to them. "Hi, Amy," he said, smiling down at her. "Sorry we're late."

"That's okay," Amy managed to say before she burst

out laughing, right in his face. "I'm sorry," she apologized. "But your hair . . . it's full of chicken feathers!"

"And that *smell!*" Palmer added, wrinkling her nose in disgust.

"Sorry about that, too," Mars said, coming up to them.

Shanon giggled. "It reminds me of the first time we all met last fall," she said. "Remember how you guys came to the costume ball wearing chicken heads? Well, this time you're wearing chicken feathers!"

"And chicken droppings!" Amy said, pointing to a spot on John's shirt.

John's face turned red. He pulled a handkerchief out of his pocket and started rubbing at his shoulder. Then Mars found a similar spot on the leg of his pants. He looked at Shanon and grinned. "You can see how desperate we were to come see you," he said. "We got here any way we could!"

"But why didn't you just come on the bus like everybody else?" Palmer demanded. "And where's Simmie? And what's Rob doing with that weird-looking boy over by the truck?"

At that moment, they all saw Rob take the dark-haired boy's arms and pull him over in their direction. All at once, Lisa screamed with laughter. "Don't you see who it is?" she cried. "It's Pee-wee Herman! Only it isn't really! It's . . . it's . . ."

"Oh my gosh!" Palmer exclaimed in horror. "It's Simmie! This is awful! Simmie, why are you dressed like Pee-wee Herman?"

Behind his Pee-wee Herman makeup, Simmie's face was bright red with embarrassment. "It's my last stunt for the Hydraulic Dudes," he mumbled apologetically. "They said I had to impersonate a celebrity. I said okay because I thought I'd get to be Robert Redford or Tom Cruise. But then they told me I had to be Pee-wee!"

As they gaped at Simmie's bow tie and short, tight suit, Lisa, Shanon, and Amy doubled over with laughter. Palmer didn't look the least bit amused, though. She'd been imagining a date with the best-looking boy in the universe, and now she was going to be having breakfast with the most famous nerd in the world!

Rob let go of Simmie's arm and walked over to Lisa. "Hi there," he said. "Sorry we were late. Our pal Pee-wee was so embarrassed about leaving our room, he made us miss the bus. We thought we weren't going to make it at all, but then that farmer came by and offered us a lift. Hope you don't mind the fragrance of chickens."

Lisa reached up and plucked a feather out of Rob's dark, curly hair. "I don't mind," she told him. "I'm just glad you made it.

Lisa looked over at Simmie in his costume and started to giggle again. "I'm glad you made him come. Having something to laugh at made me feel a little less nervous about seeing you."

"I was nervous, too," Rob said. "But now that I'm here, I'm not!"

"Me neither," Lisa said.

Rob lowered his voice and spoke in her ear. "Listen, Lisa," he said softly. "I wanted to talk to you about—"

But Rob was interrupted in mid-sentence by one of the senior girls ringing a giant bell. "Breakfast is served!" she announced. "Pick up your plates and silverware at the blue table! Get your pancakes at the red table! Form an orderly line! Come and get 'em while they're hot."

"Yeah, come on!" Amy urged Lisa and Rob. "Hurry up so we can get our own table."

Rob and Lisa followed Amy and John over to the serving tables, where several senior girls were dishing out heaping platefuls of strawberry pancakes. When they had their food, they went to join Palmer and Simmie, who were sitting at a small table in the farthest corner of the yard. As the four of them sat down, they heard Palmer trying to convince Simmie to take off his Pee-wee costume.

"At least get rid of the makeup," Palmer was saying desperately. "And that hideous bow tie."

Simmie shot a glance at his gold watch. "I can't yet," he said. "Not for another twenty-three minutes."

"He promised the Hydraulic Dudes he'd wear the costume for a whole hour," John explained with a grin. "And I volunteered to help keep him to the schedule."

"Thanks a lot, pals," Simmie said bitterly.

111

"Anything for a fellow roomie!" Mars said cheerfully, as he and Shanon came up to the table.

"Wow, are we ever lucky!" Shanon said as she sat down. "This is the only table with just eight chairs at it."

"There *were* ten," Palmer said. "I moved two of them to a different table when no one was looking so nobody else would sit with us. The whole world doesn't have to see me having a date with Pee-wee Herman!"

Simmie reached into his suit pocket and pulled out a pair of sunglasses. "Maybe no one will recognize me in these," he said, putting them on. Everyone at the table laughed. Pee-wee Herman in Polo sunglasses looked even funnier than without them!

When they'd all stopped laughing, they got busy smearing butter and pouring syrup onto their pancakes. For a while, there wasn't much talking because everyone was too busy eating. Then Rob spoke into Lisa's ear.

"I finally got that letter you wrote me about," he said softly. "You know . . . the one where you said you hated me."

Lisa almost choked on a piece of pancake. "You were supposed to tear that up without reading it!" she whispered.

"I know, but I was curious," Rob whispered back. "Anyway, I'd already gotten the whole story out of Simmie about the hazing stunts and the tricks he pulled on you." He put down his fork and frowned. "I was really mad when he told me what he'd done," he said grimly. "I couldn't believe he would go that far just to be an idiotic Hydraulic Dude."

"Didn't you get tapped for one of those societies yourself?" Lisa asked.

"Yeah, but I told them I wasn't interested. For a while, I thought I might have made a mistake, but now I'm glad. I mean at this very moment, you could be sitting next to Bozo the Clown or Donald Duck or—"

"Or Porky Pig," Lisa sputtered.

"Right!" Rob laughed.

"Poor Simmie," Lisa said. "He does look ridiculous in that outfit."

"I have no sympathy after those tricks he pulled on you! It was one thing for him to try embarrassing *me*, but to involve *you* like that was totally outrageous!"

Lisa nodded and shrugged. "Well, the Foxes have all agreed not to talk about it anymore since the subject always starts a fight. And since you knew I didn't mean what I said in that letter, I guess it doesn't matter that much."

"I guess not," Rob agreed. "Though I sure would have been bent out of shape if I'd gotten that letter out of the blue one day! I mean there I would have been, thinking things were going so well between us . . . and, you know, BLAM!"

Lisa felt a warm feeling spread to the tips of her fingers.

She smiled back. "I know," she began, just as Kate Majors came over to their table, offering second helpings on pancakes.

Lisa looked behind Kate and saw that her brother Reggie was carrying Kate's tray for her! Since Reggie usually avoided any sort of work like the plague, she knew that must mean he really liked Kate a lot. Maybe Shanon and Miss Grayson were both right, and Kate actually was a nicer person than everyone else thought!

The four boys helped themselves to several pancakes each, but the girls all shook their heads. Lisa in particular felt she couldn't eat another bite. For one thing, she was worried about bursting a seam in Palmer's skin-tight leggings. But for another, she was much too happy to even notice what she was eating.

Throughout the rest of the breakfast, everyone talked about the crew races that would be coming up soon. Both Ardsley and Alma Stephens would be involved in separate races, and each school was invited to watch the other's competition.

Before long, a senior came around to clear the table. "What are we supposed to do now?" Shanon asked her.

"We didn't plan anything but the pancakes," the girl said. "So I guess you just have free time for a while. Make the most of it while you can, because you *know* it won't last very long!"

They all laughed and pushed back their chairs. Without a word, Lisa and Rob began slowly walking up the path that followed the river toward the boathouse. All at once, Rob came to a stop. He stepped off the path and stood in the shadow of an enormous old oak tree.

"Hey, guess what!" he exclaimed. "If you stand just right, this tree almost gives you some privacy!" He motioned for Lisa to come over and stand close to him. "See what I mean?"

Lisa nodded without saying anything. Then Rob cleared his throat. "I just wanted to say a few things to you while we have a chance," he said softly. "First of all, about your letter . . . the nice one, I mean. It was great. It really made me happy when I got it and . . ."

"And?" Lisa whispered. Her heart was beating so fast she could hardly talk.

"And I feel the same way about you. I really think you're terrific. The fact is, I'd been wanting to write you about it for a long time, but I just didn't have the courage. I was afraid you might write back and say you only wanted to be friendly pen pals, that you were writing me so you could practice your handwriting, or whatever."

"What a dumb idea." Lisa giggled. "Handwriting practice! That's the stupidest thing I've ever heard!"

Rob shook his head and threw out his hands in mock dismay. "Now you're calling me stupid!" he exclaimed, pretending to be wounded. "It's enough to make me change my mind!"

Lisa caught her breath. "Change your mind about what?" she asked in a small voice.

Rob was fumbling in his pocket. "About asking you to wear this," he said softly, holding out his hand. Something small, gold, and white glinted on his palm.

It was his freshman class pin!

Suddenly, Lisa was so happy she felt dizzy. For a minute she couldn't speak. She just stood where she was, staring down at the pin in Rob's hand.

After a minute, Rob tapped her on the shoulder. "Earth calling Lisa," he said gently. "What are you thinking about? Do you want me to put this thing away? Have I just made a total jerk out of myself?"

"No!" Lisa said sharply. "That is," she said in a softer voice, "what I really mean is *yes*. Yes, I'd love to wear your pin. Thank you."

She reached out and took the pin from Rob's hand. When she tried to pin it onto the collar of Palmer's red shirt, her hands fumbled with the clasp. Rob reached out to help her, and the pin fell to the ground. They both laughed and bent down to hunt for it in the grass. When they finally found it, Lisa grasped it in her hand. "I think I'll just hold on to this for a while," she said. "It might be safer if I wore it on a chain or something."

"Just as long as you wear it," Rob said. He stood up and then reached down to pull Lisa up beside him. When she was on her feet, he kept holding onto both her hands. "I couldn't believe it the first time I met you last fall," he said. "You'd been writing such terrific letters—and then you turned out to be so pretty, too!"

Lisa blushed and stared up at Rob's face. How could Palmer ever have called Rob homely? she wondered. With his dark hair and eyes and his tall, strong body, he was the best-looking boy Lisa had ever seen!

Rob bent over and slowly brought his head down toward Lisa's. Her heart started thudding so wildly, she thought she might fall over backwards. But suddenly, Rob jerked his head away from her. "Hi there, Simmie!" he said, in a loud, annoyed voice.

Lisa whirled around and looked behind her. To her embarrassment, she saw Simmie standing only a few yards away. He'd taken off his Pee-wee jacket and bow tie and managed to wash off most of his makeup, and now he looked like his normal handsome self again. Even with his Polo sunglasses on, it was clear he'd been staring at Rob and Lisa. "Don't let me interrupt anything," he said with a smirk.

"Hey, you two!" Palmer exclaimed, coming up beside Simmie, with Mars, Shanon, Amy, and John just behind her. "The rhyme goes, 'sitting *in* a tree, K-I-S-S-I-N-G'—not standing under it!"

"That's right," Simmie teased. "Shall I go fetch you a ladder?"

"What are you two doing over there, Lisa?" Shanon asked anxiously. "A teacher could come along any minute and see you!"

"Maybe they *want* everyone to see," John laughed to Amy. "Maybe we should sell tickets for this event!"

117

"Unfortunately, there isn't time," Amy said. "The chicken truck has vanished, but the Ardsley bus is waiting to take Lisa's leading man away!"

As the teasing went on, Lisa felt her face getting hot. She was embarrassed, but she kept holding on tightly to one of Rob's hands. In her other hand, she clutched his freshman class pin.

"What a bunch of Peeping Toms!" Rob said in disgust. "Is the bus really leaving already?"

"I'm afraid so, buddy," Mars said sympathetically. "They just made the announcement while you two were . . . busy."

Rob sighed and squeezed Lisa's hand. Then the two of them joined the group on the path and started slowly walking toward the yard. The Ardsley teachers were busily hustling all the boys onto the bus. All the pen pals started saying good-bye to each other.

Rob was one of the last boys to head for the bus. "Well, I guess I can't put this off forever," he said finally. "I have to get back to Ardsley Penitentiary."

"I'll still be waiting for you when you get out in twenty or thirty years," Lisa joked.

"Thanks," Rob answered. "And thanks for inviting me to this breakfast. It was incredible. Short, but incredible."

He started toward the bus and then turned around and quickly pressed a piece of paper into Lisa's hand. " 'Bye," he whispered. "For now."

Lisa held the paper tightly as she watched the bus close

its doors, turn around, and head off down the driveway. Then she opened it up and read Rob's note. Like the breakfast, it was short but incredible.

Dear Lisa,
*   You're fantastic. Let's write!*

Rob

Something to write home about . . .
five new Pen Pals stories!

In Book 4, Palmer takes up tennis so she can play in a round-robin tournament with Simmie Randolph III. But when she finds herself playing against—not with—her super-competitive pen pal, she suddenly realizes that winning the game may mean losing the boy!

Here's a scene from Pen Pals #4: NO CREEPS NEED APPLY!

Palmer and her partner, Gary Hawkins, stood across the net from their opponents—Megan Morgan and Simmie Randolph III.

A trickle of sweat ran down the side of Palmer's face. She'd never played better! Tennis no longer seemed like hard work; it didn't even seem like something she had to think about. All the work she'd done with Lisa and Coach Barker was finally paying off. Her timing and reflexes were perfect!

But suddenly a noise on the other side of the court broke her concentration—an angry groan from Simmie as he let a point slip by! Palmer blinked and looked over at him. Simmie's green eyes were flashing angrily, and his face was red with exertion and frustration. She remembered something he had said to her earlier: "Whenever I lose, I really hate the person who beats me. . . ."

Palmer kept playing as well as she could, but inside she began to feel shaky. Now she had to work to keep her eye on the ball, and she could actually feel Simmie glaring right at her.

Despite the look in Simmie's eye and the commotion in Palmer's mind, the two couples were still playing about even. If Palmer slipped ever so slightly, Gary Hawkins's excellent timing made up the difference. On the other side, Simmie's partner Megan was playing well, too. The audience seemed mesmerized as the ball went back and forth over and over again.

The two teams traded games until the score was 6–6. Then it was time for the "sudden death" tie-breaker. The first team to score five points would win.

Again, the players seemed perfectly matched, and soon it was 4-all. But then, playing for the final point, Megan suddenly made a weak shot. The ball sailed straight toward Palmer. It was the chance she and Gary needed to win the tournament.

For a fraction of a second, Palmer's eyes left the ball and met Simmie's angry gaze. And suddenly she knew—if she made the winning point, it would be the end of everything. He would never speak to her again, let alone take her to the

Ardsley dance or be her pen pal. Her eyes came back to the tennis ball floating toward her. The moment seemed like an eternity. It was an easy shot. She knew she could make it. With her racket held back, Palmer ran to meet the ball. . . .

The whole point of learning to play a game was playing your best, Palmer knew. That's what Coach Barker had taught her. That's what her mind told her, too. But her heart was saying something different. . . .

Heart or mind—which would Palmer heed?

PEN PALS #5: SAM THE SHAM

Palmer has a new pen pal. His name is Sam O'Leary, and he seems absolutely perfect! Palmer is walking on air. She can't think or talk about anything but Sam—even when she's supposed to be tutoring Gabby, a third-grader from town, as part of the school's community-service requirement. Palmer thinks it's a drag, until she realizes just how much she means to little Gabby. And just in time, too—she needs something to distract her from her own problems when it appears that there *is* no Sam O'Leary at Ardsley. But if that's the truth—who *has* been writing to Palmer?

PEN PALS #6: AMY'S SONG

Amy and her pen pal John have written a song together, and it's great—too bad they can't agree on the lyrics. Amy finally gives in because she values John's friendship too much to risk losing it. Meanwhile, all the girls are buzzing about the class trip to London, but Amy is most excited of all. One of the Ardsley boys has arranged for her to sing the song in a London club. "Just don't forget my words," John warns Amy. But in all the excitement, that's exactly what she does. Will John ever forgive her?

PEN PALS #7:   HANDLE WITH CARE

Shanon is tired of standing in Lisa's shadow. She wants to be thought of as her own person. So she decides to run for student council representative—against Lisa! Lisa not only feels abandoned by her best friend, but by her pen pal, too. While the election seems to be bringing Shanon and Mars closer together, it's definitely driving Lisa and Rob apart. Lisa's sure she'll win the election. After all, she's always been a leader—shy Shanon's the follower. Or is she? Will the election spoil the girls' friendship? And will it mean the end of Rob and Lisa?

PEN PALS #8:   SEALED WITH A KISS

The Ardsley and Alma drama departments join forces to produce a romantic rock musical, and Lisa sees the perfect chance to spend more time with Rob. She auditions and lands a place in the chorus. But it's Amy who gets a leading role—opposite Rob! And when Amy's character has to kiss Rob's character, Lisa can't help wondering: Is Amy only acting? Or is she really falling for her best friend's pen pal?